VICTORIA MARY SACK...

(1892–1962) was born at Knole in Seve... were first cousins, her father being the ... her mother the illegitimate daughter o. Lionel Sackville-West and the Spanish dancer Pepita. Knole was to be an abiding passion throughout her life, the inspiration of much of her writing, and the source of great sorrow when, as a woman, she was unable to inherit it on her father's death. Vita was educated at home, except for three years spent at a school in London where she came to know Violet Keppel (later Trefusis) with whom, from 1918–21, she was to have a passionate affair.

In 1910 Vita met Harold Nicolson, the young diplomat whom she married three years later. In 1915 they bought a cottage two miles from Knole where they planned their first garden; three years later Vita Sackville-West's first novel, *Heritage*, was published. A distinguished novelist, poet, short-story writer, biographer, travel writer, critic, historian and gardener, her novels include *The Edwardians* (1930) and *All Passion Spent* (1931), both published by Virago, and *Seducers in Ecuador* (1924); of her poetry, *The Land* (1926) was awarded the Hawthornden Prize and *The Garden* (1946) won the Heinemann Prize.

During the 1920s her close and influential friendship with Virginia Woolf was at its height, culminating in the publication of Virginia Woolf's novel *Orlando* (1928), a celebration of her friend. In 1930 Harold and Vita bought Sissinghurst Castle in Kent, where they created their famous garden. A Fellow of the Royal Society of Literature and a JP for Kent, Vita Sackville-West was made a Companion of Honour in 1948. She died at Sissinghurst, after an operation for cancer, at the age of seventy.

VIRAGO
MODERN
CLASSIC
NUMBER

175

NO SIGNPOSTS
IN THE SEA

V. SACKVILLE-WEST

With a New Introduction by
VICTORIA GLENDINNING

FOR EDIE

Published by VIRAGO PRESS Limited 1985
41 William IV Street, London WC2N 4DB

First published in Great Britain by Michael Joseph Limited 1961

British Library Cataloguing in Publication Data
Sackville-West, V.
    No signposts in the sea.
    I. Title
    823'.912[F]   PR6036.A35

    ISBN 0-86068-578-0

Printed in Great Britain by Cox and Wyman
at Reading, Berkshire

Introduction

This is V. Sackville-West's last novel. It is set on board ship. Vita
was a seasoned traveller by sea, at first because in her young days
there was no other way to go, and later because she loathed the
very idea of flying. On the seventieth birthday of her husband
Harold Nicolson, a group of his friends presented him with a large
cheque; he and Vita decided to spend it on a luxury cruise. From
then on until her death they joined a cruise ship every winter—six
voyages in all.

Both of them extracted a book from these excursions; Harold
Nicolson's *Journey to Java* celebrates their first cruise, and provides
among other things an affectionately humorous picture of how
Vita conducted her life on shipboard. Vita's own characteristics
—such as her way of making a cluttered 'home' out of her cabin,
her passion for the markets and bazaars at their ports of call, and
the importance she gave to the letters that awaited her at each
landfall—are also echoed in *No Signposts in the Sea*, in the character
of Laura. Laura's detachment, and her power of 'making you
believe (alas how fallaciously!) that you were the only person
whose society she desired' are also Vita's own.

But the novel is dedicated 'For Edie', and Vita said that Laura
was an invention, 'except in so far as she bore certain
resemblances (mental not physical) to the Edie of the dedication'.
Edie Lamont, a painter, lived not far from Sissinghurst. Vita and
she became close friends shortly before the Nicolsons' first cruise
and she became, in the last few years of Vita's life, the person she
loved most outside her family. On the last unhappy cruise in 1962,
when Vita was mortally ill (though her cancer was still

undiagnosed) Edie Lamont accompanied them.

Before they set out on the second cruise, to the West Indies and South America, Vita had thought of 'a novel I might write on the boat'; she referred to it in her diary as 'Edmund and the gold casket'. 'Edmund' was indeed to be the central character of the book. But that year she fell seriously ill on the boat, and could not work at all. She was never to enjoy uninterrupted normal health again.

It is giving away no secret of the plot, since it is revealed early in the novel, to say that her narrator Edmund is under sentence of death: his doctor has given him only a few months to live. Both Vita and Harold were thinking apprehensively of the end of life, their own and each other's. 'It is awful the way we are getting preoccupied by death', Harold wrote to her in 1959. But he did not think that 'whoever remains behind will ever doubt the love of the other, or reproach themselves for not having assured the other of their devotion . . . it is a small comfort, but a comfort'— and one of which Edmund in the novel will be deprived.

The cruise on which the story is based was their third; in early 1959 Vita and Harold sailed on the *Cambodge* to Port Said, Aden, Bombay, Colombo, Singapore, Saigon, Manila and Yokohama— and then back to Marseilles, where they had joined the ship. During the voyage, Vita was longing to start her novel but 'can't make even a beginning'. It was a conversation with a fellow passenger, Sonia Orwell, that may have triggered her off. She wrote in her diary: 'After lunch Sonia Orwell talks about George Orwell to whom she was married only three months; she says neither of them had any idea he was so near death.' A few weeks later, on the way back, Harold reported to their son Nigel that Vita 'has actually STARTED ON HER NOVEL'.

It was going, she wrote in her own diary, 'in a direction I didn't intend'. Her own physical decline played its part. Working on the book back at Sissinghurst, she felt isolated and depressed—'I can't see an end to this illness'—and the novel became the repository of her personal summings-up of life, love, sex, and work. She finally finished it on their next voyage, on the way to South Africa; it was published in early 1961 when they were afloat again, off to South America. Rarely has the writing of a novel been so intimately bound up with its setting.

The local colour of shipboard life is, naturally, drawn from direct observation and experience. During the voyage, according to Harold, he and Vita were 'aloof but courteous'; Vita in fact spent much of each day working in her cabin, emerging at mealtimes and in the evening. Like Edmund in the novel, Vita loved to pass islands, remote and never to be visited; like Edmund and Laura, she and Harold watched sunsets, sunrises and storms together; like Edmund, they were caustic about overweight passengers who exposed their ageing flesh to the burning sun by day and propped it against the bar by night.

The exquisite place, half-Oriental and half-Spanish, where Edmund and Laura grow close to one another, seems to be based on Macao, the stopping place that Vita loved most on the 1959 cruise: 'I don't think H. and I have ever spent a happier two days.' Her description to a friend of the 'eau-de-nil house among banyan trees and tamarinds, looking out over the fishing fleet towards China', is very like the account in the novel. Her mention, in the novel, of the baroque ruined church on the hill—St Paul's basilica?—would seem to confirm this identification; though Macao is, of course, Portuguese and not, like the paradise in the novel, Spanish.

The travelogue and reportage, vivid though they are, constitute only the surface of the novel—which is, in effect, a meditation on how life should be lived, through the medium of Edmund's diary. He is rethinking all his values: 'I am at sea in more ways than one.' He has brought a crate of books with him; the diary is interspersed with quoted extracts in verse and prose, without attributions. Identifying these—they range from Thomas Wyatt to Thomas Browne and Jeremy Taylor, and on to G. Lowes Dickinson—is part of the pleasure and frustration of this novel for the committed reader.

Edmund is not wholly satisfactory as a creation. He is a man of humble origins who has become an opinion-former, as leader-writer for what is obviously *The Times*. He is a man fascinated by politics, and has written a famous book, *Some considerations on the ethnical problems of the Middle East*. Yet we are asked to believe what is almost impossible, given his position and achievements—that he has never before left the shores of England.

Unlikely though this may be, it does have a non-realist significance—in that never before has Edmund risked the deeps of emotion and introspection, or ventured into the territory of subjectivity. Faced with death, and Laura, he discovers needs and feelings he has never acknowledged.

It is in his conversations with Laura that the true topics of the book emerge. Chief of these is love. Before he has fallen too deeply for Laura, Edmund is dismissive about sexual love as 'monotonously repetitive' and quickly forgotten. He has no experience of companionate love; and he assures Laura he is incapable of jealousy.

Later, they discuss marriage. Anyone familiar with Vita's and Harold's theories about that institution will recognise Laura's prescription for success: mutual respect and independence, separate bedrooms, and a shared sense of values. Laura pays tribute to the strength of a long marriage, in a way that echoes

Vita's often expressed feelings: 'There is nothing more lovely in life than the union of two people whose love for one another has grown through the years from the small acorn of passion to a great rooted tree. Surviving all vicissitudes, and rich with its manifold branches . . .'

To this extent, the author endorsed her own experience of marriage, with gratitude. But she has the courage to probe further. Laura, the 'perfect woman', talks later about the electrifying experience of being *in* love: 'For the time being nothing matters but the one thing. *Parceque c'était lui; parceque c'était moi*', she says, using the formulation of Montaigne's that Violet Trefusis and Vita had repeated like a charm, years before.

Laura describes a total love, comprising sexual love and companion love bound up in the one person—something that had eluded the author, on account of her duality. If she ever knew total love of that kind, says Laura, 'I should be utterly faithful, and I should presume the same fidelity in the other person'.

This novel is heavy with the 'if only' of Vita's divided life and divided love. Because of her nature, and Harold's, this absolute, integral commitment was a luxury denied to her. At the end of her life she apprehends it as an ideal, in a way she would not and could not have done earlier.

The novel also touches on other things that deeply mattered to her—on the excitements and disappointments of writing, for example: and, for the first and last time, in prose at any rate, on love between women. This last is approached indirectly, with Laura reporting on lesbian love apparently at second hand. The concord between women who love one another, she has heard, can 'approach perfection', marred only by jealousy. The lesbian lover is always afraid that 'the natural thing', i.e. heterosexual attraction, would win in the end. But jealousy, as Edmund discovers, is part of the absolutism of all passionate love, for everyone.

No Signposts in the Sea is not a great novel. The third main character, Colonel Dalrymple, is pretty much of a stock figure. The attitudes to Jews, 'natives' and social manners reveal the limitations and orthodoxies that Vita's class and age group had imposed upon her. Not for one minute can one believe that Edmund springs from the background attributed to him; and, in order to serve the ironies of the plot, he is made to be peculiarly slow in the uptake on a crucial matter.

More impressive is the clean structure of the book, which is simple and coherent and easily supports the discourse that is superimposed on it. The topics themselves are important, and universal. Vita Sackville-West had always wanted to write an honest novel about marriage; and she had never published any prose work that dealt directly with what had made and marred her own marriage—her sexual and emotional complexity. *No Signposts in the Sea* is the nearest she got to either. It exhibits her innate seriousness, her strengths as a craftsman and her limitations—heartbreaking, to her—as an artist. It is a moving and original book: it is her fictional testament.

Victoria Glendinning
London, 1984

NO SIGNPOSTS IN THE SEA

WE have now been at sea for three weeks. It may
have been a foolish idea of mine to follow Laura, but
I never hesitated when I realised I could watch her
daily for two months, perhaps more, perhaps less.
It was the solution.

She betrayed no surprise when first she met me
on deck, but then she never does betray her feelings.
Tall and cool in grey slacks and a white shirt, she
merely raised her eyebrows and gave me her usual
charming smile of recognition.

'Why, Edmund!' she said. 'You never told me I
was to have the pleasure of your company. How
far are you going?'

'All the way.'

'And back?'

'Perhaps not back.'

Another woman would have enquired further
into my intentions if only to show a conventional
interest. That was not her habit. She has a disconcerting way of letting a subject drop, or is it because,
reserved herself, she respects the reserve of others?
I noted once more as I had noted many times before
that she managed this feat without conveying any
impression of indifference. Intrusive curiosity was
not for her, but I knew that had I chosen to enlarge
upon my plans, I could with certainty have counted

on an attentive listener, bending her grave grey eyes upon me, for she possessed more than any other woman the supreme element of charm: the power of making you believe (alas, how fallaciously!) that you were the only person whose society she desired. It was perhaps for this reason that she drew many confidences she did not invite, as unintentionally as a magnet draws steel filings.

*　　　*　　　*　　　*

In the shipping office, when I went to book my passage, they must have thought me extremely vague. Even now, I scarcely know our destinations.

> Where lies the land to which yon ship must go?
> Festively she puts forth in trim array,
> And vigorous as lark at break of day,
> Is she for summer seas or polar snows?

*　　　*　　　*　　　*

It is a strange life that one lives at sea. Here we are, afloat, a community of some fifty passengers, linked only by small occurrences and daily happenings—'Did you see the whales spouting this morning?'—knowing nothing of one another, in most cases not even our names, nothing of our backgrounds nor of the complications of our lives. Little groups inevitably coalesce, the young people dance together, the elderly form chess-table or bridge-table friendships. For my part I have scarcely sought to disentangle them; my identifications consist mostly in avoidances. There is the lonely questing English-woman whom I instantly recognised as a menace;

8

I, the detached male, was an indicated prey. Not bad-looking, and carefully made-up, she disguises the poverty of her mind and no doubt the starvation of her heart by a bright, eager manner, as an indifferent poet will seek to add interest to his lines by laying them out in the shape of a wine-glass, or an indifferent pastry-cook decorate his cakes with pink sugar roses. Then there is the repellently uxorious German couple who despite their middle-age seem unable to keep their hands off each other. Heaven knows there is enough to lay hands on, those rolls of fat, those bulges of flesh, which must still hold some allurement. His little pig eyes roam concupiscently over her vast thighs, reddened by the sun, revealed by the tightest and briefest of shorts.

Le dégout de la chair. . . .

And the three giant Jewesses who lean so close, gossiping, that it looks as though their noses must get hooked together.

'It is lucky for some people,' I say to Laura, 'that they can live behind their own faces.'

She reproaches me for intolerance, little knowing that she herself sets my standard, provides my measuring-rod.

*   *   *   *

She likes talking to people, or perhaps it would be truer to say that they like talking to her, for I cannot imagine her seeking anybody out. I see her in the most incongruous company, persons in whom I could not have believed her to take any interest—

desiccated old maids, bouncing young men; it is not difficult to strike up an acquaintance on board ship, but how do their revelations so quickly attain so personal a note? She entertains me with potted biographies of our fellow-passengers.

'Do you see that rather distinguished-looking grey-haired couple over there? They are going round the world for the oddest reason: to discuss whether they shall or shall not divorce.'

'It seems an expensive way of settling one's difficulties—cheaper to sit down and thrash it out at home. But how do you know?'

'They told me. She told me first, and he told me afterwards.'

'What an extraordinary thing to confide to a stranger.'

'Oh, within the first five minutes. Is it any more extraordinary than the things that people will say to one in railway carriages? That their husbands beat them, for instance, or that their son is in prison for forging a cheque.'

'People don't say that sort of thing to me, Laura. You must give them inviting glances.'

'I assure you I don't. I won't deny that I am interested. It is rather like watching fish in an aquarium, such diversity, you know—one could no more invent so many different situations than one could devise so many sorts of fish. Think of the fantasy of hippocampus, or of the tiny creature with a row of neon lights down its back, or that frilly

10

object that looks as though it were made entirely of beige chiffon.'

Be that as it may, she certainly has the gift of involuntarily drawing people out. I taxed her with fraudulence, for although, as she says, she is interested, it is in a very detached way.

'They don't know that you regard them as specimens. You ought to be a novelist—it is a novelist's interest.'

'Not wholly,' she said. 'It is true that I have little patience with the spoilt, the self-pitying, the futile. They make me want to shake them into some sort of reality. I would far rather listen to someone like, say, my cabin steward.'

'Tell me about your cabin steward.'

'Well, his home is in an Italian hill-village where he has a consumptive wife whom he loves and three consumptive children. He has a week's leave while the ship turns round—that's three times a year. When he gets back he never knows how many of his family he will find alive. In the five years he has been on this ship he has never once had time to go ashore—there is always too much to do. His day begins at six and ends at ten, and when he has finished with the cabins he has to help in the dining-saloon. What a life, Edmund! perpetually clearing away the remains of other people's food, emptying other people's ashtrays, and making other people's beds. The flowers and champagne that he has to carry in, represent more than his total earnings. He told me all this in the most matter-of-fact

11

way, without a hint of complaint, and when I tried to express some sympathy he merely said that life was like that.'

It strikes me as somewhat ironical that the one person who will never confide in Laura is myself.

*   *   *   *

There are good moments when I am lulled into contentment with my lot. Laura and I landed on an island where industry is unknown and Nature so kindly that the inhabitants are satisfied to live on the fruits of the earth and the fish of the sea, rather than exert themselves in clangorous factories or in the competition of prosperity. With what contempt I should have regarded them in my Grub Street days! My sense of values has indeed undergone a reversal. Can it be that I shall yet have time left me to learn wisdom?

> Oh sweet woods the delight of solitariness!
> How much do I like your solitariness,
> Where man's mind hath a freed consideration
> Of goodness to receive lovely direction . . .
> Here nor treason is hid, veiled in innocence,
> Nor envy's snake's eye finds any harbour here,
> Nor flatterer's venomous insinuations,
> Nor cunning humorist's puddled opinions,
> Nor courteous ruin of proffered usury,
> Nor time prattled away, cradle of ignorance,
> Nor causeless duty, nor comber of arrogance,
> Nor trifling title of vanity dazzleth us,
> Nor golden manacles stand for a paradise.
> Here wrong's name is unheard, slander a monster is.
> Keep thy sprite from abuse, here no abuse doth haunt.
> What man grafts in a tree dissimulation?

12

Whether it be the cause or effect of their happy-go-lucky life I cannot tell, but the physical beauty and grace of these islanders appeared to my inexperienced eyes as something out of this world. Civilisation had not grimed the golden skin of these young men, and as for the women in their soft many-coloured draperies they were like flowers walking. Men and women alike, in every poise, every gesture, moved like trained dancers. I recalled the rush-hour in London stations, the hordes in soiled raincoats pouring out of the suburban trains, alighting before the train had stopped, running, dodging to get faster through the crowd, the strained faces, the shabby brief-cases, the pushing to get into the Underground, the queues waiting in the drizzle for the bus—'No more room!' This island was a lyric poem replacing cacophony.

*   *   *   *

Laura and I went with an English friend, a voluntary exile in this Paradise. He drove us for miles beside deserted beaches where the little grey crabs scuttled in the white sand. I had never seen Laura as childishly gay, nor had I ever felt so close to her, and I realised for the first time how greatly our apprehension of people depends on the variation of conditions under which we see them, and thought it possible that we may never truly perceive them at all. Supposing for instance that we were suddenly furnished with instruments of perception other than eyes and language, even as some birds

13

and insects mysteriously communicate, they might appear totally different from our conception, as different as a grass-stalk appears to a minute fly or to me. Has it not been said that if we could truly behold our wooden table, instead of solidity we should see nothing but a congery of holes actuated by perpetual movement? But apart from crazy fantasies, what do I know of Laura? Not even her age; thirty-five at a guess. Our acquaintance goes back a year, limited to London drawing-rooms, to an occasional visit to her own flat, always with others present, and to one happy day at Kew. I know the outward facts of her life: that she is a widow, much courted but (so far as I know) indifferent to the devotion she inspires. Has she a secret lover? If so, she keeps him very dark; but then she *would*. (I must not let this idea gain possession of me.) For the rest, we have always got on very well, oh yes! very well. I think I may say she quite likes me; at any rate she always greets me as though I were welcome, and once when she found herself next to me at dinner in London she said comfortably 'How nice this is, Edmund,' and I thought she really meant it.

*   *   *   *

Our friend stopped his car by the roadside and invited us to follow him along a track leading into a forest of greenery. It elated me to feel that we were thousands of miles from our normal haunts. Accustomed only to seeing Laura in London, I noted as a revelation how nimbly she moved over the

14

rough ground, refusing a helpful hand and saying with a laugh that she had been born among the moors of Cumberland. Shall I gradually obtain other fragments of information?

The track led us up and down until we came to an open shelter with a reed roof, in a clearing. Here squatted four men round a charcoal brazier, their brown bodies naked save for a loincloth. They were working on tortoiseshell, cutting, scraping, and filing against the hardened ball of their foot, with the dexterity of a lifetime, surely an ancient craft which could never be replaced by machinery and which involved the seemliness of all manual skill. They took no notice of us, never even glanced up, but continued with the manipulation of their pieces and the selection of their tools from the brazier, bending the shell into the shape required, moulding it, splicing it so smoothly that no join was perceptible, polishing it with chalk and sandpaper till from the rough material it emerged into the finished satiny texture of the familiar brown.

'So some of them do work for a living,' I said.

'Yes, but they will work no longer than they need to earn enough for the day's keep. Then they will down tools and go home.'

'No ambition? No thought of the future?'

'None.'

Once, I suppose, I should have been shocked. Now, I was filled with amused delight. Meeting Laura's eyes, I saw that she was in sympathy.

A whisper came through the trees, no more than

15

a faint susurration at first, increasing to a patter, a downpour, as the tropical shower descended on the palms and the broad banana leaves, running in rivulets, splashing, bringing with it a refreshment and a scent made up of wet greenery and soaked earth. Drops rebounded from the leafage in tiny rainbows. Not for years had I been aware of such a sense of peace and satisfaction.

The shower having ceased as abruptly as it had begun, we strolled away, the grasses washing tepidly against our ankles. Laura said, 'To think of those cigarette boxes, those dressing-table objects, those paper-cutters, ending up in Asprey's front window in Bond Street!'

'It's very cruel really,' said our friend, negligently, as though it were a thing he took for granted. 'They prise the shell off the living tortoise and then throw the creature back, raw, into the sea, in the hopes that it will survive to grow another shell for their benefit.'

'And does it?'

'About one in a hundred does.'

*   *   *   *

Must one always be struck down, after a moment of elation?

*   *   *   *

Illusion is best. Can it be I, the realist, writing these words? See how kindly the mist transforms an ugly prospect. There upon the shore across the bay at the foot of the mountains rises an ethereal city; those pearly bastions surround a Crusader's castle, and from those tall towers float the black pennants of Saracen defenders. Do not tell me that those bastions are galvanised oil-drums, nor that those towers are factory chimneys emitting a plume of dirty smoke. I prefer not to know.

*   *   *   *

Do not tell me either that Laura can never, in the common sense of the word, be mine. I accept, I am resigned, but there is no need to rub it in. I like to hoodwink myself that in these last weeks of my life I shall draw nearer to her than if she lay nightly in my arms. There was a time when I loved women, and crudely took what I wanted and what they were willing to give, but even in those days I fancy that a worm crawled, unacknowledged, in the recesses of my mind, prompting me to dissatisfaction and to a shrug of the shoulders and a dismissive 'Well, that's that. Another episode ended.' A sadder and more fastidious philosophy—not, I think, without its elegance—rounds off in finality my earlier discontent, though it may well be that, desiring the unattainable, I have persuaded myself that even the desirable is better left unattained. There is a certain *chic* in voluntary renunciation. Thus I argue that physical passion is best forgone; left, unfulfilled, to the imagination. For what is the reality? Nothing remains. That animal instinct which brooks no denial, hurling us together in the hours of darkness,

17

that pathetic short-cut suggested by Nature the supreme joker as a remedy for our loneliness, that ephemeral communion which we persuade ourselves to be of the spirit when it is in fact only of the body—durable not even in memory! There are moments of such seeming perfection when, clinging to one another, we murmur 'This we must remember . . . this we *shall* remember . . .' but we never do. Monotonously repetitive, carnal delights all merge, and when the impulse has died away—after a year, five years, ten years?—all recollection becomes impossible.

Grey ashes after the fire.

Perhaps the ideal would consist in spending one perfect night and then never again, so that it stood out in memory as sharp as a Greek temple seen against the sunrise. No blurring of detail, no pain of diminution.

> Fill a vessel to the brim,
> And you will wish you had stopped in time;
> Temper a sword-edge to its sharpest,
> And you will find it soon grows blunt.

*   *   *   *

I said something of the sort to Laura; it arose quite naturally, I think, out of some book we had both been reading.

'What a paradox of refinement!' she said. 'Cynicism or idealism—which? But haven't you dwelt on only one aspect of love? Haven't you left out all question of companionship?'

'Perhaps I have never had the good fortune to know it.'

Again that disconcerting trick of hers: she did not pursue the subject. Surely my answer might have provoked some show of interest? I was left wondering what her own experience had been: had she loved her husband—lost everything in losing him? I cannot believe her to be as cool and impersonal as she appears. How does she contrive to be so aloof and yet at the same time so inviting? Shall I force her confidence, without betraying my own? What would be the effect on this very strange sense of nearness which, were I given to such fancies, I should call a mystical bond? Luckily, I have a living warning daily before my eyes, in the shape of a Miss Corcoran who has already hinted that she is a Taoist and seems as determined to impart her views on the Occult Wisdom of the East as I to prevent her.

*   *   *   *

Our fellow-passengers really impinge very little, or is it that I am no longer so good a mixer as my profession once obliged me to be? Ever since we all first assembled for lifeboat drill, travestied and deformed in our panoply of padded orange breast-plates and white tapes, far less dignified I swear than the horsemen of Pizarro quilted against the arrows of the Incas, I have been unable to regard my fellow-mortals as other than grotesques. What can have come over me? It is as though I had been

19

suddenly endowed with X-ray eyes, and could see a group of human beings only in terms of their insides; I see the coils of intestines, the sack of the stomach, the bellows of the lungs, the busy heart, the bladder filling and emptying. I become aware of the terrible dependence on the body, on some mean invisible organ altering a man's whole outlook on life. Looking down at the lower deck on stormy days, I reflect that those miserable huddled figures, green in the face and lost to all respect for decency, care neither whether they or their loved ones die. I know perfectly well that under torture I myself should betray my dearest—if I had one.

Men, that look no farther than their outsides, think health an appurtenance unto life, and quarrel with their constitutions for being sick; but I, that have examined the parts of man and know upon what tender filaments that fabric hangs, do wonder that we are not always so; and considering the thousand doors that lead to death, do thank my God that we can die but once.

*   *   *   *

Many jokes were bandied about at the lifeboat drill. Much hilarity was caused by the struggles of the huge German woman who had been mistakenly supplied with a life-jacket designed for a child. We were all new to each other then, and it seemed a good opportunity for making acquaintance in the same way as it is permissible to address a complete stranger at a fancy-dress ball. The jokes were mostly concerned with the possibility of meeting again, similarly attired, but in deadly earnest. It was taken

20

for granted that this rather ridiculous precaution would never need to be put into practice. 'No nonsense about women and children first,' said a tall Colonel, pretending to glare round. 'How many days in an open boat before we start eating the youngest?' someone asked the deck-steward, who received the pleasantry gloomily; he had heard it all before. Somebody started singing:

> On tira à la courte paille
> Pour savoir qui, qui, qui serait mangé . . .
>
> Le sort tomba sur le plus jeune,
> Le sort tomba sur le plus jeune . . .
>
> Ce s'ra donc lui qui, qui sera mangé,
> Ce s'ra donc lui qui, qui sera mangé . . .

*　　　*　　　*　　　*

Now, when passengers joining the ship after a call at other ports are summoned by siren and gather together in groups to have their tapes adjusted, we the old-timers lie back in our deck-chairs to watch them, much as we used in our school-days derisively to watch the new boys at the beginning of term.

*　　　*　　　*　　　*

It is amusing to observe a batch of new passengers coming on board. From the superiority of the upper deck one gazes down upon the quay-side swarming with native porters and Europeans, distinguishable

21

from the idle crowd of sight-seers who have come to stare at the ship for want of anything better to do. What a medley of noise and colour! Then comes the rush as the gangway is lowered; everyone wants to be first, though there is no conceivable reason for hurry; women hesitate and struggle back, convinced that they have lost their luggage; men enter into argument with the officers in their cool white ducks. The emigrants lugging their poor bundles are directed to a secondary gangway near the stern; they turn this way and that, like panic-stricken cattle. A tall black-bearded man in a red turban clutches a small girl swathed in blue muslin. A Buddhist priest with shaven head and saffron robe falls flat as he stumbles over a rope. A lost child sets up a howl. Is it possible that all this pullulating humanity will ever be sorted out?

It seems like a microcosm of everything that is happening all over the world.

Behind them the great sheds of the warehouses are disgorging their bales and packing-cases, to be picked up by giant hooks dangling from the cranes, lifted, and soaring up to be deposited into the gaping pit of the ship's hold. I never cease to marvel at the nice precision of these machines, such delicacy combined with such power, and all controlled by a tiny man aloft in a tiny cabin. These are the moments when one has to salute the ingenuity of the human brain. These obedient giant toys, that can equally scoop up a five-ton weight or a motor-car and sling it through the air as though it were

22

made of tin, when it looks as foolish as any object deprived of its rightful means of progression.

Machines. Down on the quay writhe black-jointed pythons feeding oil into the ship, and again I think of the vast oil combines netting the world and of the residue of countless primeval fish turned to this strange service by the inventiveness of man.

Behind it all, as a back-cloth, towers the massive mountain. Stupid and brainless, it has defeated the encroachment of man's city by the very steepness of its escarpment; the city is restricted to the foreshore. Yet even here man has vulgarly conquered: a cable railway transports tourists in little cages to the summit, where they may buy panoramic postcards and drink Coca-Cola.

Meanwhile the ship pollutes and dishonours the sea with refuse—floating orange-peel, sodden cartons, bobbing bottles, stale bread. The gulls swoop and cry over this bounty.

Then comes departure. Loud-speakers warn all visitors to go ashore. Streamers of coloured ticker-tape frailly link the vessel to the land, and human heart to human heart, before they snap as the ship detaches herself slowly from her moorings and moves out towards the open upon the renewal of her voyage. Wave goodbye! Who knows how many of you will ever meet again?

Through the rainbow of gay motley paper I discern a woman, left behind, weeping.

*   *   *   *

In the dining-saloon I sit at a table with three other men, Laura sits some way off with a married couple and their daughter. I can observe her without her knowing, and this gives me pleasure, for it is as in a moving picture that I can note the grace of her gestures, whether she raises a glass of wine to her lips or turns with a remark to one of her neighbours or takes a cigarette from her case with those slender fingers. I have never had much of an eye for noticing the clothes of women, but I get the impression that Laura is always in grey and white by day, looking cool when other people are flushed and shiny in the tropical heat; in the evening she wears soft rich colours, dark red, olive green, midnight blue, always of the most supple flowing texture. I ventured to say something of the kind to her, when she laughed at my clumsy compliment and said I had better take to writing fashion articles instead of political leaders.

*   *   *   *

The tall Colonel whose name is Dalrymple seems a nice chap. He and I and Laura and a Chinese woman improbably called Mme. Merveille have made up a Bridge-four and thus beguile ourselves for an hour or so after dinner while others dance on deck. The Colonel, who is not too offensively an Empire-builder, sometimes tries to talk to me about public affairs; he says he used to read me, and is rather charmingly deferential, prefacing his remarks by 'Of course it's not for me to suggest to *you* . . .'

and then proceeding to tell me exactly how he thinks some topical item of our domestic or foreign policy should be handled. He is by no means stupid or ill-informed; a little opinionated perhaps, and just about as far to the Right as anybody could go, but I like him, and try not to tease him by putting forward views which would only bring a puzzled look to his face. Besides, I do not want to become involved in discussion. I observe with amusement how totally the concerns of the world, which once absorbed me to the exclusion of all else except an occasional relaxation with poetry or music, have lost interest for me even to the extent of a bored distaste. Doubtless some instinct impels me gluttonously to cram these the last weeks of my life with the gentler things I never had time for, releasing some suppressed inclination which in fact was always latent. Or maybe Laura's unwitting influence has called it out.

Yet I realise now that I was always fascinated by the question of man's desire for power with a capital P. As leader-writer to one of the weightiest of our national newspapers, I suppose that I myself was guilty of the same obsession. Gratification came to me, especially in times of crisis, from the thought of sober men at their breakfast tables, unfolding the great sheets and attentively reading the words I had typed over-night. 'Let's see what Carr has to say.' Anonymous though my contributions might be, the name of their author was an open secret. Oh yes, I had influence, and I protest that I used it conscientiously, never playing on emotion and often taking the line I knew would lead to resentment. I had early learnt the lesson that if you dare to make yourself sufficiently provocative you end by gaining respect, having earned a reputation for moral courage—'Can't say I agree with Carr today, but at least he's never afraid to speak his mind.'

My editor would send for me.

'They won't like this, you know, Carr.'

'Sorry, they'll have to take it.'

'Well . . . All right, if you say so.'

*   *   *   *

This was power of a sort, bringing its minor as well as its major rewards. I frequented houses where I, a man of the people, should never have expected an invitation. Charming women flattered me, and prominent men asked my opinion. I don't think I am more of a snob than most people, perhaps rather less, and can honestly say that I esteemed my admission to these inner circles for the sake of its value to my work and profession. It enabled me to consort freely with members of influential political families. I lived politics, I breathed politics, I dreamed politics. My love affairs, kept in a separate compartment, were simply the diversion of a normal healthy man. Over and over again I was invited to stand for Parliament, but I had created my own position and felt, rightly or wrongly and certainly conceitedly, that its solitary eminence suited me better than absorption into a party herd.

26

My old dad was always greatly amused by my social activities, of which he had conceived an exaggerated idea. Whenever I went to stay with my parents in the cottage that they firmly refused to leave although I could well have afforded to transfer them to a more comfortable home, he would say 'Been hob-nobbing with the Prime Minister lately, Ed?'

*   *   *   *

Power. The desire to lead, the wish to command. Was I being honest in telling myself that I was indifferent to honours and recognition, inspired solely by the noble purpose of devoting my talents to my country and the world? Of course I was not being honest. I liked being Edmund Carr, with a European reputation, and across the Atlantic too. Is there anything to be ashamed of in that? Even in the days of the cave, some men must have aspired to authority in the tribe. Ambition, old as mankind, the immemorial weakness of the strong.

*   *   *   *

I see now how much I passed by on my swagger road. Dismissive as a Pharisee, I regarded as moon-lings all those whose life was lived on a less practical plane. Protests about damage to 'natural beauty' froze me with contempt, for I believed in progress and could spare no regrets for a lake dammed into hydraulic use for the benefit of an industrial city in the Midlands. And so it was for all things. A hard materialism was my creed, accepted as a law of progress; any ascription of disinterested motives aroused not only my suspicion but my scorn.

And now see how I stand, as sentimental and sensitive as any old maid doing water-colours of sunsets! I once flattered myself that I was an adult man; I now perceive that I am gloriously and adolescently silly. A new Clovis, loving what I have despised, and suffering from calf-love into the bargain, I want my fill of beauty before I go. Geographically I do not care and scarcely know where I am. There are no signposts in the sea.

*   *   *   *

Is it possible that I am coming round to the point of view of the Chinese official?

To look for good not in wealth, not in power, not in miscellaneous activity, but in a trained, a choice, an exquisite appreciation of the most simple and universal relations of life. To feel, and in order to feel to express, or at least to understand the expression of all that is lovely in Nature, of all that is poignant and sensitive in man. . . . A rose in a moonlit garden, the shadow of trees on the turf, almond bloom, scent of pine, the wine-cup and the guitar; these and the pathos of life and death, the long embrace, the hand stretched out in vain, the moment that glides for ever away, with its freight of music and light, into the shadow and hush of the haunted past, all that we have, all that eludes us, a bird on the wing, a perfume escaped on the gale. . . .

*   *   *   *

What pleasure we derive from the humble workers going about their tasks: a string of brown naked fishermen dragging their nets ashore, a man

28

ploughing with oxen, a woman walking with a pitcher on her head. Her arm in its upward curve provides the handle of the pitcher. For us, speeding by, they pass in a flash of grace, while for them life goes on day after day in unconsciousness and monotony. Should we return a year hence, we should find them still poised as though time had not moved an hour.

*   *   *   *

The young moon lies on her back tonight as is her habit in the tropics, and as, I think, is suitable if not seemly for a virgin. Not a star but might not shoot down and accept the invitation to become her lover. When all my fellow-passengers have finally dispersed to bed, I creep up again to the deserted deck and slip into the swimming pool and float, no longer what people believe me to be, a middle-aged journalist taking a holiday on an ocean-going liner, but a liberated being, bathed in mythological waters, an Endymion young and strong, with a god for his father and a vision of the world inspired from Olympus. All weight is lifted from my limbs; I am one with the night; I understand the meaning of pantheism. How my friends would laugh if they knew I had come to this! To have discarded, as I believe, all usual frailties, to have become incapable of envy, ambition, malice, the desire to score off my neighbour, to enjoy this purification even as I enjoy the clean voluptuousness of the warm breeze on my skin and the cool support of the water. Thus, I imagine, must the pious feel cleansed on leaving the confessional after the solemnity of absolution.

*   *   *   *

Sometimes Laura and I lean over the taffrail, and that is happiness. It may be by daylight, looking at the sea, rippled with little white ponies, or with no ripples at all but only the lazy satin of blue, marbled at the edge where the passage of our ship has disturbed it. Or it may be at night, when the sky surely seems blacker than ever at home and the stars more golden. I recall a phrase from the diary of a half-literate soldier, 'The stars seemed little cuts in the black cover, through which a bright beyond was seen.' Sometimes these untaught scribblers have a way of putting things.

The wireless told us today that there is fog all over England.

*   *   *   *

Sometimes we follow a coastline, it may be precipitous bluffs of grey limestone rising sheer out of the sea, or a low-lying arid stretch with miles of white sandy beach, and no sign of habitation, very bleached and barren. These coasts remind me of people; either they are forbidding and unapproach-able, or else they present no mystery and show all they have to give at a glance; you feel the country would continue to be flat and featureless however far you penetrated inland. What I like best are the stern cliffs, with ranges of mountain soaring behind them, full of possibilities, peaks to be scaled only by the most daring. What plants of the high altitudes grow unravished amongst their crags and valleys? So do I let my imagination play over the recesses of Laura's character, so austere in the foreground but nurturing what treasures of tenderness, like delicate flowers, for the discovery of the venture-some.

My fellow-passengers apparently do not share my admiration.

'Drearee sorter cowst,' said an Australian. 'Makes you long for a bit of green.'

*   *   *   *

Darkness falls, and there is nothing but the intermittent gleam of a lighthouse on a solitary promontory.

*   *   *   *

We rounded just such a cape towards sunset, the most easterly point of a continent, dramatically high and lonely, a great purple mountain overhung by a great purple cloud. The sea had turned to a corresponding dusk of lavender. Aloof on the top, the yellow light revolved, steady, warning; I wondered what mortal controlled it, in what must be one of the loneliest, most forbidding spots on Earth. Haunted too, for many wrecks had piled up on the reefs in the past, when there was no beacon to guide them.

31

The Colonel joined us.

'How would you care for that man's job?' he said.

'I suppose he gets relieved every so often?'

'On the contrary, he refuses ever to leave. He is an Italian, and he has been there for years and years, with a native woman for his only company. Most people would think him crazy, but I must say I find it refreshing to think there are still a few odd fish left in the world.'

This is the unexpected kind of remark that makes me like the Colonel; there is a touch of rough poetry about him. I like also the out-of-the-way information which he imparts from time to time without insistence; he has travelled much, and has used his eyes and kept his ears open. I have discovered also that he knows quite a lot about sea-birds; he puts me right about the different sorts of gull, and tells me very nicely that that couldn't possibly be an albatross, not in these waters. The albatross, it appears, follows a ship only to a certain latitude and then turns back; it knows how far it should go and no further. How wise is the albatross! We might all take a lesson from him, knowing the latitude we can permit ourselves. Thus, and no further, can I follow Laura. I suspect also that there is quite a lot of lore stored away in the Colonel's otherwise not very interesting mind. Laura likes him too, and although I prefer having her to myself I don't really resent it when he lounges up to make a third.

*   *   *   *

32

In all this great serenity of ocean it is seldom that we espy so much as another ship; the jolly dolphins and the scratchy little flying-fish have the vast circle all to themselves, 'the Flying Fish, who has a part with the birds,' and doubtless are glad to see the last of the monster which bears us into and out of sight. Our wake closes up and we might never have been. But it does happen from time to time that an island appears on the horizon, nameless to us and full of mystery, the peak of a submarine mountain range, lonely, unblemished, remote. Does one like islands because one unconsciously appropriates them, a small manageable domain in a large unmanageable world? I cannot tell why it should give me such a queer sensation to reflect that that island has always been *there* (unless indeed it be no more than the work of the patient coral) and will be *there* still, should I return to find it waiting for me. It is the same sensation as I have experienced in looking at a photograph of, say, some river valley of innermost China, and seen a boulder, and thought that if I could find myself transported to that spot I could touch the reality of that particular piece of rock. . . . It is *there*. For *me*. I could sit on that very boulder. I explain myself badly, and it is not a sensation I could expect anyone save Laura to understand, but of such incommunicable quirks is the private mind made up.

Well, the islands. I divert myself by inventing the life upon them, and am amused to find my imaginings always turning towards the idyllic. This is the new Edmund Carr with a vengeance. If we have seen a skiff sailing close inshore, I follow the fisherman as he beaches his craft in the little cove and gives a cry like a sea-bird to announce his coming. His woman meets him; they are young, and their skins of a golden-brown; she takes his catch from him. In their plaited hut there is nothing but health and love.

One night we passed two islands, steeply humped against faint reflected moonlight; and on each of them, high up, shone a steady yellow gleam.

'Not lighthouses,' I said to Laura, 'Villages.'

We gazed, as the ship slid by and the humps receded into the darkness and even the lights were obscured by the shoulder of a hill, never to be seen by us again. So peaceful and secret; so self-contained.

One of the ship's officers joined us, off duty.

'Yes,' he said, following our gaze. 'One of them is a leper colony and the other a penal settlement.'

God, is there no escape from suffering and sin?

*   *   *   *

Laura and I amuse ourselves by watching for the green flash which comes at the instant the sun disappears below the line of the horizon. This does not happen every day, for the sky must be entirely clear of cloud and clouds seem very liable to gather along the path of the setting sun, but we are as pleased as children when our game succeeds. Laura claps her hands. Only a second does it last, that streak of green light; we wait for it while the red ball, cut in half as though by a knife, sinks to its

34

daily doom. Then come the twilight colours of sea and heaven (we have discovered the fallacy of saying that darkness falls suddenly in these latitudes, at any rate on sea level), the wine-pink width of water merging into lawns of aquamarine, and the sky a tender palette of pink and blue. But the green flash is our chief delight.

'Crème de menthe,' says Laura.

'Jade,' I say.

'Emerald,' says Laura. 'Jade is too opaque.'

'Vicious viridian,' I say, not to be outdone.

'You always did lose yourself in the pleasure of words, Edmund. Say green as jealousy and be done with it.'

'I have never known the meaning of jealousy.'

*   *   *   *

I am sorry to see the sun go, for one of the pleasures I have discovered is the warmth of his touch on my skin. At home in London I never noticed the weather, unless actually inconvenienced by fog or rain; I had no temptation to take a flying holiday to the South and understood little when people spoke or wrote of sunlight on white walls. Now the indolence of southern latitudes has captured me. I like to see dusky men sitting about doing nothing. I like the footfall of naked feet in the dust, silent as a cat passing. I like turning a corner from the shade of a house into the full torrid glare of an open space. I put my hand on metal railings and snatch it away, burnt. But it is seldom that I go ashore.

*   *   *   *

I would never have believed in the simple bliss of being, day after day, at sea. Our ports of call are few, and when they do occur I resent them. I should like this empty existence to be prolonged beyond calculation. In the ship's library stands a large globe whose function so far as I am concerned is to reveal the proportion of ocean to the land-masses of the troubled world; the Pacific alone dwarfs all the continents put together. Blue, the colour of peace. And then I like all the small noises of a ship: the faint creaking, as of the saddle-leather to a horseman riding across turf, the slap of a rope, the hiss of sudden spray. I have been exhilarated by two days of storm, but above all I love these long purposeless days in which I shed all that I have ever been.

*   *   *   *

When that Harley Street door shut behind me and I walked away under sentence of death, I wondered quite dispassionately how best to arrange what remained of my life. I remember I went and sat in St. James's Park, while two courting pigeons prinked and preened round my feet. It was the queerest afternoon I ever spent. I knew then with certainty that I might drop at any moment, and that for as long as I continued to draw breath it would be in company of that secret knowledge—secret, for my first determination was not to tell a soul, and indeed there was nobody to tell, with my parents dead, no close friends, and no woman in my life since I had known Laura.

36

Let me pity others, myself not pitied be.

Once before, when bitten by an adder, suffocating, fighting to breathe, yet in full possession of my wits, not undermined by a long illness, I had been convinced (not unreasonably, as I was later assured) that within a few minutes I should cease to exist. The sponge would have passed across the slate. To this day I can recall the clarity of my thought, a compound of regret and curiosity, regret for a life which had treated me well, curiosity as to whether I should pass into extinction or into some unimaginable continuation. An agnostic, I had no belief in immortality; it would be interesting to find out if I had been right or wrong. And really that was all there was to it. No fear; I swear I felt no fear.

And as I sat in St. James's Park, faced by the same prospect with the only difference that it might be less imminent, forced to consider the one common certitude, again I felt no fear. Vexed I was, and thought what a pity, but my frame of mind took chiefly the form of surprise at our normal optimism in keeping the image of Death away. That it would come we knew, but how or when seemed inapplicable to ourselves. Our personal death appeared safely far off. Now here was I, not contemplating death by accident in times of peace or by violence in war when even the soldier believes that not he but the next man will be hit, but death, my own death, impending, immediate, through some mere failure of function in the body. One has to be practical. I had to consider how to deal with the situation. Should I resign from the paper or carry on with my work to the end? It was then that I discovered as in a moment of inspiration the desire to be done with all that and to plunge into the luxury of exploring the opposite aspect of the world. *'En renonçant au monde et à la fortune, j'ai trouvé le bonheur, le calme, la santé même la richesse; je m'aperçois que qui quitte la partie la gagne.'* Well, I could not hope for *santé*, and as for *richesse* I had earned enough for my needs, and no one dependent upon me.

*   *   *   *

It so happened that I was dining out that night and the talk turned upon euthanasia. The usual arguments were advanced: very dangerous . . . mercenary heirs . . . ah, but there were safeguards, the consent of the subject, the opinion of two doctors, three if you like . . . doctors sometimes made mistakes . . . miraculous cures . . . wonderful discoveries in medicine and surgery. . . . Some woman inevitably said, What about animals? You wouldn't keep an animal in pain, would you? so why a human being? and some High Anglican said, What about the immortal soul? Someone else recalled the old joke about the parlour-maid opening the door to say, 'Please, sir, the euthanasist has come'—and what would you feel then? Congenital idiots and senile decay—what was to be done in such cases when the consent of the subject could not be obtained?

You know the sort of thing.

Our hostess was pleased, as hostesses are always pleased when a topic turns up to keep the conversation animated for the rest of the evening.

They appealed to me.

'Come on, Carr, what's your attitude? Supposing you knew yourself to be smitten by a mortal disease? You might write us an article one day to brighten up the Silly Season.'

I went home marvelling at how little even good friends know of what is really passing in each other's minds.

*   *   *   *

Some weakness in myself made me ring Laura up next morning and ask if I might come to tea. Simply, I wanted to sit with her for an hour in her quiet room.

It was then that I learnt her intention of setting out on a long voyage, and knew in a flash that my own meagre future was decided.

*   *   *   *

A couple of days sufficed to set my affairs in order, for I had never cluttered myself up with possessions and was perfectly willing to put my rooms into the hands of house agents for sub-letting as they stood. I supposed that I must make a will, but after distributing amongst a few friends such books as I didn't want to take with me I was brought up against the difficulty of inventing a residuary legatee. Laura obviously had everything in the material sense

39

that she needed. So I dashed off a paragraph leaving my furniture and such money as might remain after booking my passage and providing myself with an adequate sum for current expenses, to an impoverished youth of whom I held a high opinion on the staff of my paper. I grinned as I signed my name and thought of his astonishment on being apprised, some day, of this windfall.

A flattering consternation greeted me at the office, but when I pointed out that I had worked for over ten years since the war with scarcely a break they conceded that I was entitled to a spell of indefinite leave. My place would be kept open for me. They would pay me a retaining fee of half my usual salary during my absence. No? They would pay me the whole of it if I liked. No? That was very high-minded of me, and would be duly reported to the board of directors. Would I at least promise not to accept other employment when I got back? Good! They wished me, most cordially, a happy carefree journey and drank my health in the special 1850 brandy.

I grinned again as for the last time I unfolded the august sheets in the train to Dover and read a boxed footnote stating that Mr. Edmund Carr was on holiday but would resume his articles on his return to this country.

No greater or more unprecedented compliment could be paid me than this breach of their policy of anonymity.

*　　　*　　　*　　　*

For one thing I am grateful: I shall bring no grief to anyone by my passing. My friends would probably set me down as a hard man, but I was always haunted on behalf of others by the thought of leaping danger and felt their troubles as keenly as I could have felt my own. Little they knew it. I had a morbid conception of life as a path one travelled complacently, with slight ups and downs perhaps, but on the whole smooth and predictable, and then suddenly opening a chasm not easy to bridge. It might be some vicissitude of fortune, it might be personal disaster, a crippling accident or the loss of the beloved; whatever it was, it came unannounced and must be surmounted with some fund of courage one did not know one possessed. I used to look at people whom I knew to have been struck by some such calamity, and wonder what private anguish they had suffered and how they could continue apparently unchanged. The craziest ideas came to me: that a friend from whom I had just parted would walk into a lift shaft when the lift was not there, or open his front door to find the fatal telegram lying on the mat. In the stolid and unimaginative person I knew myself to be, this abnormality struck me as peculiar in the extreme. I wonder now whether my own destiny cast a shadow of prescience ahead of my confident steps? or are we perhaps none of us as sane as we like to imagine?

For another thing I am grateful: I shall be spared old age. I know that it comes imperceptibly—*chacun croit que la jeunesse durera bien jusqu' à l'année prochaine*—but the sneaking hints must make themselves felt; nothing very precise at first; one finds oneself going more slowly upstairs, stooping to retrieve a pencil produces a twinge in the back, one coughs, one wheezes, one says 'What?' more frequently; young men take to calling one 'Sir.' All very comic, no doubt, but in the last resort tragic. I have lived my half-century; I have no need to anticipate a less pleasurable quarter.

*   *   *   *

Death intermedleth, and everywhere confounds itself with our life: declination doth preoccupate her hour, and insinuate itself in the very course of our advancement: I have pictures of mine own, that were drawn when I was five and twenty, and others being thirty years of age, which I often compare with such as were made by me as I am now at this instant. How many times do I say, I am no more myself; how much is my present image further from those than from that of my decease? It is an over-great abuse unto nature to drag and hurry her so far, that she must be forced to give us over, and abandon our conduct, our eyes, our teeth, our legs and the rest, to the mercy of a foreign help and begged assistance.

*   *   *   *

One small deception I have practised: I have not informed the ship's doctor of my condition. To have been refused a passage at the last moment would have been beyond endurance, and this is the custom on certain shipping lines; they don't like deaths at sea. The ship's doctor can do nothing for me, and as I am neither an expectant mother nor an obvious invalid he pays no more attention to me than to anybody else. I have however taken the precaution of leaving an envelope addressed to him, containing the report I got my own doctor to write out; it will be found in my pocket-book, and save all the bother of an inquest. I have studied it, and marvel that such unintelligible jargon should represent what is going on inside a man.

It was with some amusement that I submitted myself to compulsory vaccination against smallpox and inoculation against cholera, typhoid and yellow fever. Much good may it do me! but anyway it satisfied the authorities that I should remain in a presentable state of health.

I have read somewhere that in certain South American rivers myriads of microscopic fish fasten themselves to a submerged body, and in a twinkling nibble until nothing is left but the clean white skeleton.

*   *   *   *

Laura gave me a large diary on New Year's Day, by which time we had reached the southern warmth and she had had the opportunity of observing me gazing idly at the sea.

'Don't thank me for it,' she said; 'it was pressed upon me as a parting present and you will make better use of it than I.'

'Scribble, scribble, Mr. Gibbon?' I said, much touched all the same.

*   *   *   *

So I write in it, all anyhow, and irrespective of dates, a volume never to be filled. She little knows how queer it is to open its pages at random, a day to a page, and to fall upon some distant date, say November 21st, or even a date in March, April or May. Or even next month, or next week, or tomorrow. Or today.

There will be a total eclipse of the sun, visible as a partial eclipse in Great Britain. There will be new moons and full moons, punctual and recurrent, predictable through this year and millions of years hence.

I have never troubled to keep a diary, but my little pocket engagement-books have given me similar pangs as I leafed through their New Year blankness. What will have happened by then? In the old life, my queries were general rather than personal; I don't think I was ever much concerned with myself. Now, I hit on my birthday, July 1st, and smile, I hope not too wryly.

The triteness of these reflections is redeemed only by their new poignancy.

$*$ $*$ $*$ $*$

How safe we seem, on this ship equipped with charts, wireless, radar, and even an apparatus which draws with a pen a continuous picture of the sea-floor beneath us.

By reason of the long navigation, and want of food and water, they fall into sundry diseases, their gummes waxe great, and swell, and they are faine to cut them awaie, their legges swell, and all the bodie becometh sore, and so benummed that they can not stirre hand nor foot, and so they die from weakenesse, others fall into flukes and agues, and die thereby.

No, my journey cannot be described as adventurous, except perhaps as an adventure of the spirit.

* * * *

'What a pity,' I said to Laura, 'that we should live on such a well-mapped planet. Don't you envy the early explorers who never knew what might be round the next corner? Fancy coming suddenly on the Grand Canyon when you had no idea of its existence.'

'My dear Edmund, I should never have taken you for a romantic.'

'No? Well, perhaps you are right. But I am taking a holiday, you see, when I find a lot of queer fish rising to the surface from the bottom of one's mind. One has leisure to make up for lost time. I begin to suspect that it is possible to concentrate too greatly on the mundane side of life.'

'And has it taken you all these years to come to that conclusion?—In any case,' she added, as though fearing that her question might have been too personal, too indiscreet, and also that my answer might involve her into betraying her own opinion, 'how can we get on, in the state our civilisation has reached, without concentrating on what you call the mundane side? Heaven knows we make enough muddle of it, but at least we try, and some day our descendants may emerge to find—how shall I put it? that some sort of order has been settled out of confusion.'

'In short, the noble savage is no longer a practical proposition?'

'I don't fancy that you would like him very much, at close quarters.'

'But then I don't like that big business man either—the one you call the Merchant of Alexandria —with his triple chins and his cigar, or the Texan oil king who boasts that he could buy out the Sultan of Kuwait if he were so minded. I don't like the exploitation of Nature—shafts sunk in search of valuable minerals in splendid mountains, hideous cities loading the earth, cranes and derricks disfiguring the coast, power stations where the nightingale should be singing beside a waterfall.'

'You do surprise me. I should have thought you had an admiring eye for the achievements of man.'

'Yes? Perhaps I am inconsistent—such a luxury, sometimes, to allow oneself a riot of inconsistency. I came on this trip for that express purpose. I am discovering that one of our many problems is the almost schizophrenic rift between our desire for civilisation and our desire for what Miss Corcoran would call the Return to Nature. There is a desert-islander in all of us, mostly unavowed. Until recently I never suspected his existence in myself.'

'Perhaps the artists and the contemplatives alone have resolved that problem. Yet without civilisation,

Edmund, you would have progressed no further than cave paintings or tom-toms. No Rembrandt, no Beethoven, no St. Mark's in Venice. No Venice.'

'No Sheffield either, no Chicago with its slaughter-houses.'

'But your islander made his knives, or arrows, as best he could; and as for the slaughter-houses of Chicago, do you really imagine that primitive man was any less cruel, driving herds of bison over the cliffs of the Vézère to smash themselves for easy capture on the rocks below? No, Edmund. I am afraid that man today is merely an extension of what man always was, only more complicated. A logical progression, that's all.'

*   *   *   *

Having finished with boat-drill, today we had Man Overboard practice. I had been writing in my cabin, when I became aware that the ship was swinging round in a most unwonted way; we were three days out from any port, and had been proceeding undisturbed on our straight course across an empty ocean. I went up on deck, for one's curiosity about anything unusual makes investigation as impossible to resist as, on dry land, it is impossible to resist answering an importunate telephone. We were describing a huge circle in the midst of the blue platter of the sea, our curved wake creating a kind of lagoon without a ripple, and out in this lagoon bobbed a little red flame trailing a wisp of smoke. An excited little boy, dancing up and down, pointed

47

it out to me. 'There he goes, mister, see? Oh, I do hope he drowns before they can reach him.'

Apparently they had no intention of trying to reach him; no lifeboat was lowered; they contented themselves with watching the canister carried further and further away on some unseen current. It all seemed to me as unintelligible as many other things in life. One could hope only that it made sense to someone in authority. Meanwhile it was pitiable to see that small object struggling to survive, quaking and abandoned in an inexplicable waste; the flame dwindled once, and I thought it had been extinguished, but it revived in the diminished flicker of a last determination. Then it came to the edge of the lagoon, was buffeted by the ridge of our wake, tossed desperately for a moment, and was gone for ever.

There are no tombstones in the sea.

         *   *   *   *

This morning we anchored in a bay about a mile from the coast, and idly watched a barge making its way towards us from the small port, accompanied by a fleet of skiffs in which the native merchants were raucously crying their wares. I took the opportunity of looking round at our fellow-passengers, all assembled, for anything in this existence is an excitement and a diversion. Not many of them are travelling for pleasure, as Laura and I. The majority are men, of varied nationality, mostly on Government service, or mining engineers, or regaining their job with an oil company, or working on estates up-country; I find them not uninteresting, but listen to their talk through a haze of unreality. Once, I should have been avid for the information they could give me, first-hand, practical, and hard-headed. The women are their counterparts, all looking as though they had spent too long in hot countries and had lived in too small a community; they have a faintly rapacious air, nor does it take much imagination to picture the jealousies and rivalries which must go on between them on their various stations and plantations. Even here, on board, the hierarchy obtains. The purser said to me, 'We should like to ask Mrs. Drysdale to present the prizes for the Bridge tournament, but we feel we must ask the Senior Military Lady.'

I expect he is right. The Senior Military Lady has a mouth like a trap.

For the rest, there are the inevitable missionaries of both sexes, bent on interfering with the beliefs of other people. I make an exception for one jolly old French priest who took me aside and with a wink showed me a Simenon disguised between the covers of an ostensible breviary. 'One cannot be pious all the time—eh?'

There are four nuns. I understand that they are making for some highly dangerous spot in the Far East, and certainly they seem to be getting into training for mountainous tracks, for regardless of the fact that they belong to the second class they have adopted our deck for their twice-daily constitu-

tional. Round and round they tramp, in their flat
black boots, the wind disarranging their coifs and
blowing their skirts up in a way that no holy
woman's skirt should blow. Their lips move inces-
santly in some inaudible prayer. On Sunday morn-
ings I see them at Mass in our transformed saloon,
and sometimes I have sighed, envying them.

*　　　*　　　*　　　*

Of course people come and go; we discard some,
and acquire others. I think of those who have left
us, returning to their jobs with no prospect of
leave for another two years, three years, four years,
and I watch the new-comers, wondering what turn
of destiny has moved them on to another spot of
the earth's surface, which they will find exactly the
same as the one they have quitted. The same
bungalow, the same work for the men, the same
housekeeping for the women, the same investigation
of the new neighbours, the same parties, the same
factions, the same surreptitious back-biting. There
will be a club-house, with a tennis-court, and ice
chinking in a gin-and-tonic at sunset.

I particularly enjoy watching them when the sea
is rough, making the ship heel over and forcing
them to lean in attitudes not at all accordant with
the angle of the floor, or into taking quick little
runs and fetching up with hands splayed against the
opposite wall. I like seeing the Texan Oil King made
a fool of by something stronger than himself. I like
it less when the eager Englishwoman bumps into

me and I have to catch her to save her from falling. Laura, who teases me about her, says she does it on purpose.

Their occupations on board? This is still a holiday, a prolongation of the more perfect holiday at home. They converge together in little groups, talk, play draughts, backgammon, chess, cards, do cross-word puzzles, sleep; and, more, energetically play deck-tennis and ping-pong. (I rejoice especially in the sight of two young priests playing ping-pong in their long black cassocks.) A scatter of obsolete magazines lies about; they turn the pages, look at the illustrations, and after this intellectual exertion wander off, saying with a wink, 'A little spot of shut-eye, I don't think.' Later, there is a good deal of perching on high stools at the bar, when the chaff becomes more hilarious and the women's evening dresses seem even lower than they were the night before. Busts bulge, and shoulder-straps look perilously in danger of slipping off.

When I imparted some of my observations to Laura I got snubbed as I deserved. I had no right, she said, to dismiss people in a lump. I must learn to discriminate. Many of these men were highly efficient and intelligent in their profession. Some of them were genuinely keen, glad to be going back to their jobs. I should be a better mixer and not judge by appearances.

I retired, abashed.

*   *   *   *

I had forgotten—how could I?—the sun-bathing. I can find humanity tolerable when it is dressed, or even partially dressed when it is very young with its figure unimpaired by the million meals it must have consumed since it was born, but what I cannot abide is the spectacle of stout, elderly men with the curls greying on their chests, protruding stomachs, and skin the colour of a letter-box, exposing their persons, their hands folded complacently over their navels. They lie about, hour after hour, great porpoises, great barrels of gross solidity. When they walk their flesh wobbles. As for the women . . . these ladies who in the seclusion of their homes would never dream of appearing without a dressing-gown, make as offensive an exhibition of themselves as the men. What strange aberration is it that seizes people the minute they come within sniffing range of salt water?

*   *   *   *

Our pause outside the little port had drawn most of them to the rails. Boys were diving for coins tossed to them in the clean ripples, little naked boys bronze as pennies, supple, amphibious, shaking the water out of their hair, grinning up at us and clapping their hands in an invitation for more largesse. There was a counter-attraction too: one of the ship's officers had let down a fishing-line, and as I watched it tautened; he hauled, a dangling object was hoisted up, lifted over the rail, and landed on deck. Everyone crowded round to look. Pale pink and opalescent, the infant shark thrashed about, the hook and bait still in its mouth, helpless, suffocating, struggling to escape. It could not understand. Its glaucous glazing eye rolled pitiably, in appeal. Everybody thought it very funny, especially the children who pranced and shrieked with delight and hoped its antics might be prolonged.

I spoke to a man standing beside me.

'Oughtn't they to kill it?'

He looked at me in surprise.

'It's dying anyhow. Ugly little brute. These diving boys, you know, they take no notice of the sharks, yet one snap of the jaws would have a foot off them in a twinkling. Yes, and a leg too. The water turns pink in a minute. I've seen it happen. Here's one at least that won't grow up to make any mischief.'

The little shark was taking a long time to die. Its movements became feebler, but still the urge to live was potent, in the twitching of the tail and the enfeebled opening and shutting of the gills. A convulsive movement every now and again showed that there was still determination in the creature, a reluctance to relinquish life, a desperate hope of regaining its element. Now, in its death-throes, it lay as the butt of its fellows of the same creation. After all, it was by pure chance that any of us had been born human, not spawned as sharks. We had no choice.

I saw the tall Colonel pushing his way through the crowd.

53

'Here, that's enough,' he said. 'Better put the brute out of its misery,' and with one stamp of his heel on the head the entertainment was finished. An 'oh' of disappointment went up from the children, especially the boys.

The Colonel and I strolled away together. Unusually moved by this incident, he was in an expansive mood.

'Can't stand the sight of a beast in distress,' he said. 'We know we've got to destroy some of them, and I don't hold any particular brief for sharks. But to see that poor little devil gasping its life out, with everybody standing round laughing at it. . . . You know, I used to go on safari once but I gave it up. I didn't like bringing down wild creatures which had just as much right to enjoy their life as I had. Ever shot a lion?'

'Good God, no,' I said, with a sudden vision of Printing House Square.

'It's worse to wound one,' he said reminiscently. 'Of course, to shoot a charging buffalo, that's different: it's your life or his. Damned difficult, too, to hit him in the right spot. And there's a certain satisfaction, I won't deny, in seeing that murderous thing the size of a locomotive coming at you, and seeing it crumple up just before it reaches you, all because you have plugged the shot into the right square inch. It was your life, or his. He had the brute force, and you had the skill. And then you know, Carr, one used to enjoy the life—the freedom of it, the day's hunt, and then the camp in the evening, round the fire, whether one had brought anything down or not. Because I liked that sort of life, and wasn't really so keen on killing things, I tried doing it with a camera instead of a rifle, but then I found one's chaps, one's *shikars* and porters, hadn't the same respect for you if you just photographed things instead of shooting them dead. Funny, isn't it,' he said as though it had occurred to him for the first time, 'why people should always wish to destroy? I suppose it's an instinct we can't get away from, a sort of primitive instinct. One has to kill, in order to live. Everything in Nature kills something else in Nature in order to survive. So I suppose one has to accept it, for better or worse. How do you sort it out, Carr? You're a brainy chap; I'm not.'

I was touched by this sudden outpouring. I liked the man more and more. I tried to draw him on.

'I am afraid,' I said, 'that my life has been very tame compared with yours.'

'Ah, but then you've got it up here.' He tapped his forehead. 'No, I think what brought my sporting days to an end was when I went out after seals with some fisher chaps off Labrador. Splendid chaps they were, tough as you make them, and didn't care if they'd got ice stiffening their beards or sweat running off their faces. When they weren't sealing, they were trawling in those waters, and you need to be tough for that.'

'Tell me about the sealing.'

'I enjoyed parts of it immensely. There one was, on a lonely ship, stuck in the pack-ice creaking and groaning all round you, and at night your green and red navigation lights would be reflected in the ice, the only colour as it seemed in that white world. I liked all that part of it. But then when the red became splashes of blood instead, I didn't like it so well. You see, seals are trustful creatures, and will come slithering right up to you to discover what you are. Have you ever seen baby seals? Very soft and inquisitive. The men would sometimes make a pet of one of them, and play with it.'

He paused, and I could see that he was thinking back. I could imagine him, adopting a little seal himself, as he might play with a puppy, getting fond of it, handling it with his gentle hands, training it to bounce a ball on its nose, having fun together.

'Those were harp-seals,' he resumed in a more practical informative tone. 'They're called that, because of the harp-shaped saddle on the back of the adults. The young have thick woolly creamy coats to start with, in fact they are called Furry Whitecoats, and it is partly for the sake of that fur that they get killed within the first week of their lives. A couple of weeks later, they get killed also for the layer of fat that develops beneath the skin. It is quite easy to kill a pup: the skull is soft, and you hit it with the pole or gaff that you also use for testing the ice. That's all right, and probably the most humane way of doing it, but sometimes an inexperienced or impatient man will merely stun it by a kick on the head, and then flay the pelt while the pup is still alive and crying. They bleat some-

56

thing like lambs. I didn't care for that, or for the puzzled mother nosing at the horrid pink mess left lying about, still moving. Muscular reaction, of course, but all the same. . . .'

I waited for him to go on if he wanted to.

'I expect you think me awfully sentimental,' he said. 'I know those things have to be, so long as traders have to make their living and furriers want the pelts. But I did take a skunner against this slaughter, and also against the way bad shots who simply didn't know one end of a rifle from the other would fire at the adults, wounding but not mortally, and leaving the wretched beasts to die. They would slip off the floe into the water, and you could see the water turning pink. So, what with one thing and another, I rather gave up blood-sports.'

I thought of poor Christopher Smart's words, 'The seal, who is pleasant and faithful. . . .'

        *   *   *   *

I wonder how much Laura knows of all this? I think she would like him. She is interested in people, especially as types, and the Colonel is very much of a type, with personal differences of his own.

        *   *   *   *

Meanwhile she and I meet on our established basis.

'I hope you are duly keeping your diary in that great tome I gave you?'

'Yes, Laura, I have been most industrious, I promise you.'

57

'When we get home, would you let me read, or read to me, parts of it? As a reminder of these happy days?'

'It would have to be very carefully edited,' I replied, aghast at the idea of my jottings ever coming into Laura's hands.

'I see—you have been exercising your malice at our expense. Poking fun. Poor Miss Corcoran, poor Colonel Dalrymple, poor me. Seriously,' she said, 'I envy anybody who can express themselves on paper. Words blow away and are lost. Printed, they are preserved.'

'More's the pity, very often. But you are talking to a journalist, not to an author. Nothing could be more ephemeral than my daily scribble, ending up in the dustbin if it hasn't been used to light the fire.'

'Nonsense, Edmund, I may not know much, but I do know that your book is regarded as a classic. It made a sensation when it came out, and has remained the standard work ever since.'

'My book?' I was genuinely astonished that she should even have heard of it. 'At least don't tell me that you ever attempted to read it.'

'Indeed I did. *Some considerations on the ethical problems of the Middle East.* A most repulsive title, if I may say so, and enough to put anybody off. But what a book, my dear Edmund, a *tour de force*, a masterpiece of lucidity. And amusing. And sly. And unanswerable. Comparable only to Maynard Keynes's *Economic consequences of the peace.*'

'It wasn't very popular in certain quarters, I'm afraid.'

'I don't suppose you meant it to be. Shall you ever write another?'

'I might if I were allowed to dedicate it to you.'

She blushed; I had never seen her blush before.

'You confound me. How surprised our friends would be. But tell me something about the process of writing a book; I am ignorant, and I always feel it impertinent to question literary people. I once heard a woman ask Aldous Huxley what he was writing now, and his face was a lesson to me for ever after.'

'He was a professional novelist, which I'm not. I take it that any creative work, as opposed to my own hack effort, must be intensely private, not to be mentioned, least of all discussed. No doubt the actual process is comparable. One lives in a little world of one's own, and nothing else seems to matter. The most egotistic of occupations, and the most gratifying while it lasts. To see the pages piling up, and to live in the persuasion that one is doing something worth while. Because of course one must hold on to that conviction, or one wouldn't go on. Luckily a writer's powers of self-delusion are limitless, and oh the smugness of feeling that one has done a good day's work!'

'I see what you mean about the pages piling up—the pattern working out.'

'It is rather like building a house,' I said, getting carried away. 'Every separate word is another brick laid into place, mortared to its fellows, and gradually you see the wall beginning to rise, and you know that the rooms inside will take their shape as you intended—you feel godlike, masterful. No one can interfere or restrain; for better or worse, it is entirely your own creation.'

'You said, "While it lasts!" '

'Ah, it is heavenly while it lasts. A sort of intoxication. But there is all the difference between the conception and the completion. So much floats through your mind as you write, that never gets put down on paper, but somehow you are persuaded that it must convey its pressure to the reader. Perhaps one credits him with more perspicacity than he possesses. Or with more willingness to take trouble. The average reader skims; he does not pause to observe what you, Laura, rightly called the pattern. He does not weigh, as the author has weighed, the value of each word; he does not stop to notice in passing the subtlety of small touches by which you have endeavoured to build up your structure. Indeed one might say that it takes a writer to appreciate another writer, one craftsman appreciating the technical skill of another craftsman. But above all there is this question of *seeing*.'

'Seeing?'

'I can't think of a better word. It sounds less pretentious than vision, yet that is what it amounts to. You *see* suddenly, as in a finished picture, the entire shape and design of what you intend to do. I don't say that you ever carry it out to your satisfaction, but for one brief moment of illumination you have apprehended the unity of what you meant. That is the moment of truth, of exaltation—one of the few moments in life worth living. No matter if it lasts only ten minutes while you are soaking in a hot bath. Any artist, whether he be a writer, above all a poet, or a painter, sculptor, musician, architect, would understand what I was trying to say. It might also, I daresay, be comparable to the religious experience of the mystic. I say that without any intention of blasphemy, Laura, please believe me. I know you think me a hard-boiled materialist; I can't help that. You must blame yourself, and perhaps blame also this enchanted ship, if I let myself go as I would never have done when I had the pleasure and honour of sitting next to you at London dinner-parties.'

'Edmund, how ridiculous you are in your determination to make yourself out as a jester. Can't you drop that stunt, out here where we are God knows where and God knows where we are going to? We are not sitting next to each other at a London dinner-party. Do you really mind letting yourself go, as you say, and letting me see something of a different Edmund? Am I trespassing? That is the last thing I would ever want to do. But I do like being talked to by the other Edmund, not the Edmund of dinner-parties. The artist Edmund, the unsuspected romantic.'

'No,' I said. 'I'm afraid you have got me wrong. Sorry, Laura, to disappoint you. I have never been, and never shall be, anything but a hack-journalist.'

*   *   *   *

She little knows what it means to 'the other Edmund' to let himself go and talk to her. The other Edmund has never had such a friend.

*   *   *   *

Sometimes I come upon her traces, a cigarette case, a scarf left trailing upon a chair. For the competent woman I divine her to be, she is curiously careless of her possessions, but then none so lovable as those who are not all of a piece. These little surprises of inconsistency are endearing enough to mere affection; how much more so when one is in love!

The Colonel and I spend quite a lot of time retrieving her belongings.

*   *   *   *

And sometimes I suddenly hear her voice. This is a queer experience. I know her voice so well in the ordinary way of things, and then suddenly and unexpectedly I hear it as though I had never heard it before. It may be only six words, of no especial significance. Thus, I heard her say no, no more coffee thank you, and it was as though she had said Edmund, my darling, I love you.

Love does play queer tricks.

*   *   *   *

When it is windy she ties her head up in one of her scarves, and it occurred to me that I would like to give her one—something that she could remember me by. Native merchants cluster round the ship in their boats and display their wares on a floating pontoon at the foot of our steep gangway, tawdry junk for the most part, but highly coloured as we look down from above on the variegated frippery and the scarlet turbans of the vendors. They make more noise than a whole murmuration of starlings.

Eluding Laura, I went down into the crowd and bought my scarf. I am rather pleased with it; it is different from the ones she already has, a rich magenta with a pattern of yellow camels all over it. I now await a suitable occasion for the presentation.

*   *   *   *

Impelled by an odd desire for approval, I showed my scarf to the Chinese woman, Mme. Merveille, that exquisite little creature who has the sense not to affect Western dress but keeps to her own pretty silks embroidered with gold dragons.

'It is for a lady-friend? a gift, yes?' she said, examining it.

I could not have brought myself to say I had destined it for Laura, so I said, 'Yes, it's a gift, but not for a lady-friend. It's for my mother's kitchen-maid.' As though my mother had ever had one! Poor old Mum!

'Ah!' she said with evident relief, 'the kitchen-maid will think it lovely—beautiful. For a lady-friend, no—*quelle horreur*! This terrible colour! those camels! For the kitchen-maid you choose well.'

And she handed it back to me.

I have tied it up into knots and dropped it into the sea.

*   *   *   *

Laura is ill, and I am beside myself with anxiety. How true the clichés of language become, when one experiences them for oneself. 'Beside myself with anxiety'—I write a phrase that would once have meant nothing to me, but now it means that I really stand outside and beside myself in an agony of worry. What makes things worse, is that I have no right to enquire; I cannot interrogate the doctor, a surly man at best, when I meet him in the passage. All I get in reply to my expressed hope that Mrs. Drysdale is making good progress is a slightly surprised look and an evasive reassurance. What is he hiding from me? I do not even know what is the matter with her; I did venture to ask if it was 'flu, but he was in a hurry and muttered something about 'that sort of thing.' For all I know it may be some exotic disorder; she may be in pain, tossing, fevered, in danger even, behind that closed door.

I feel that the Colonel is sympathetic though naturally he does not say so. He waylays me to ask if I have heard how she is, and has even suggested that I might write her a little note and send it in by the stewardess. I shall take his advice—nice resourceful man.

*   *   *   *

That was the first time I had ever seen her hand-writing, for our communications in London were always done by telephone.

'Dear Edmund,' she wrote in pencil, 'how kind of you. I am much better and shall be up amongst you all again in a couple of days. Bad throat and temperature; nothing serious. No need to worry, but thanks all the same. L.'

She is now restored to me, rather pale and thin, but evidently quite herself once more. This episode has been revealing; I could not have believed I could get into such a panic. How dear she is! How deeply I love her!

       *   *   *   *

Sometimes I look at her hands and her rings; no wedding ring, I notice; it is characteristic of her to have discarded that golden symbol of chattel-dom; but several what I think are called eternity rings and one blood-red ruby. I wonder who gave them to her? Her hands are beautiful; smooth, strong, and shapely; there is something about them which twists my very entrails. I should like to take one and, turning it over, examine the back, the palm, the mysterious lines which may or may not have such significance. Does her head govern her heart? I do not know enough about this quackery. I know only that my own life-line breaks off in a very suggestive way, as a kind friend once pointed out to me. I was sceptical at the time, but am less sceptical now and should not like to discover a similar break in Laura's—unless it meant that she and I were to die together. Philemon and Baucis, that most beautiful legend of married love. Those two old people, living in their cottage in Phrygia, visited suddenly by two gods, given a wish by the gods in return for their hospitality, chose to die at the same hour, that one of them should not have the sorrow of following the other one into the grave. Lucky Philemon and Baucis! They lived, they loved, and they died, together.

Laura and I shall neither live, nor love, nor die, together.

We might, though. Shipwreck? Most unlikely. How superstitious one is, all the same. One does not believe, and yet one half believes, even as one does not believe in prayer yet one prays in moments of fear, childishly. 'Oh, please, God . . .' I know when she was ill I prayed that she might recover. The simplest words came most naturally:

Yea, and if it be but a little word of one syllable, methinks it is better than two, and more according to the work of the spirit . . . so doth a little word when it is not only spoken or thought, but secretly meant in the depth of the spirit . . . rather pierce the ears of Almighty God than doth any long psalter unmindfully mumbled in the teeth.

*   *   *   *

I wonder why I did not make better use of the past year, after I had got to know her? From the first there was never any doubt in my mind: I fell in love the first time I met her and knew it to be different from anything which had gone before.

66

There was no obstacle of health in those days, or not so far as I knew; I saw a little court of men round her, and could have joined the circle. Pride held me back. Who was I, with my lowly birth and inelegant physique, to aspire to this creature from a different world? She must always be the Princesse Lointaine and I a very unromantic version of Geffroi Rudel. Had she given me any encouragement, singled me out in any way, I might have been emboldened; as it was, I shrank from the likely rebuff. She would administer it gently, but with finality. How fortunate that I should have retained some degree of prudence! She might now in the tenderness of her conscience be blaming herself for her denial to a dying man to whom she could have accorded some months of happiness. Had she come to care for me at all she would have suffered on my behalf. Better as it is. I shall take what I can and be grateful.

*   *   *   *

How often I have wondered, what wish I would choose, if offered one wish by some god? One would be hard put to it, to know what to ask. Or have to be very quick at the uptake. A wonderful chance! You could ask the god any question, about the immortality of the soul, for instance, or the origin of life, or the origin of the Universe, and what everything meant, if anything. A comprehensive question, and I hope the god could answer it. They said of Poseidon, the Earth Shaker, that he favoured

67

his children or god-children with a special sense, a sixth sense, warning them of when an earthquake was about to take place. I don't believe it, and yet I half believe it. What does one believe or not believe? One must believe everything, or nothing. Everything is either possible, or impossible. Miracles must be credible, or incredible. Take your choice. It is simply that we have not yet found the clue; the explanation. It, the clue, must be there, probably quite simple, if only we could find it.

Everything is a miracle, if you look at it that way. Life itself, and the origin of life. What do we know about the origin of the cell, mysteriously bursting out in an unspecified moment of time from the inorganic into the organic? What made the thing suddenly start to *grow*, and turn itself into something so fundamentally different from anything (so far as we know) that had ever existed before? When did matter become life? When did life, as differentiated from matter, become mind? When, and how, did thought arise? When, and how, and at what stage of our development did spirituality and our strange notions of religion arise? the need for worship which is nothing more than our frightened refuge into propitiation of a Creator we do not understand?

A detective story, the supreme Who-done-it, written in undecipherable hieroglyphics, no Rosetta stone supplied by the consummate Mystifier to tease us poor fumbling unravellers of his plot.

*　　*　　*　　*

I never used to think about such things.

*   *   *   *

My philosophising, such as it is, has been rewarded, for she and I have been on an unforeseen jaunt by ourselves and are still laughing over it. In one of our ports of call we met a large and genial Englishman sitting in a café; recognising us as strangers and fellow-countrymen he brought his glass over to our table and entertained us with a deal of local information. He seemed to have taken a fancy to us, or at any rate to Laura, but we were both a little startled when he said, 'Look here, you two, it's all very well travelling round on a liner, but you don't see much of the out-of-the-way places. Now supposing you go off for the night to one of the islands? Your ship's in port for two days? Good. Plenty of time. You can start after lunch and be back by tomorrow evening. I promise you the place is worth seeing. Only four hours from here by launch, and it's a pretty trip. She shall pick you up at two near your gangway.'

'She?' said Laura, bewildered.

'One of our launches. They ply backwards and forwards the whole time. I'm in the shipping business here. You can have my house on the island; I'll telephone to warn the houseboy. He and his wife will look after you. Just tell them what you want. No, don't thank me, it's quite usual. Do them good to have something to do. They speak enough English, by the way, and a little Spanish.'

'Spanish?'

'You'll see why when you get there.'

'But really . . .'

'Now that's all fixed,' he said, 'and no arguing.'

*   *   *   *

So we went. I did take the precaution of asking our Captain if he had ever heard of the man—I didn't want Laura kidnapped—and he roared with laughter.

'Lord bless you,' he said, 'his name's a household word all over this ocean. Mad as a hatter, rich as Croesus, and the best heart in the world. Take my advice and accept his offer.'

I did also take the further precaution of pointing out to Laura the interpretation that our fellow-passengers might put on our expedition.

'The man took it for granted that we were married,' she said.

'I don't believe he gave it a thought, one way or the other. But all the old pussies on board know we're not.'

'Well, do you mind?'

'Not if you don't.'

'Besides,' said Laura sensibly, 'we need not tell them we have been spending the night alone together in an empty house. They'll assume that we have gone to an hotel, and surely two grown-up people can do that quite respectably if they want to? We're not answerable to them—or to anybody.'

I had one more hesitation, which I could not

impart to Laura. Supposing I were to be stricken down? But the temptation was too great, and I persuaded myself that Fate would be kind.

*   *   *   *

From the moment we left I felt as though we had been taken in charge by a benevolent deity, our Englishman, and were being led by the hand through the landscape of a fairy-story. All responsibility was lifted from us; we had only to follow where we were directed. The native crew received us on board the little launch with smiles and courtesy; I noticed that one of them held his hand, palm downwards, against the lintel lest Laura should knock her head as she descended the steps into the cabin, a refinement of good manners. But we could not for long remain in the cabin, which indeed we had entered only at the invitation of this sailor, who appeared to be a kind of steward concerned solely with our comfort and who indicated to us with charming hospitality the drinks and cigarettes laid out on the table; we were soon on deck again, supplied now with the softest of cushions, watching the mountainous coast glide past as we threaded our way between islets large and small. A faint mist shrouded the outlines, a blue haze spreading a veil over reality. Back in the stern a boy perched, singing to himself a little song, wistful and sad; he seemed to have no connexion with the launch and no reason why he should be there; it was as though a bird had alighted for a rest. Dusk began to fall; I wished never to arrive; I wished to continue for ever between land and water in a dream region so wild and beautiful.

*   *   *   *

The house when we reached it was not at all what I had expected, in so far as I was by then capable of expecting anything. That phrase 'rich as Croesus' had disturbed me slightly, and I suppose I anticipated a luxurious villa with a cocktail bar in the drawing-room and carved wooden figures of Negroes holding electric lights. It was, on the contrary, simple to the point of austerity, with white-washed walls, red-tiled floors, large arm-chairs of rattan, and plain serviceable furniture of a peasant type. From the entrance hall and up the staircase drifted the scent of burning joss-sticks, and that was the Orient, but in the same hall a door stood open on to a purely Spanish patio with pots of camellias standing about, and a little fountain splashing into a basin.

'Laura,' I said, 'where on earth are we?'

We had been welcomed by the house-boy, smiling from ear to ear, and in the background hovered his wife, a gazelle-like young woman of incomparable slenderness, dressed in the ankle-length coat, rose-red, and split on either side up to the waist, revealing the long white silk trousers. Behind her crowded four small children, who, seeing Laura smile at them, came forward to make us solemn bows, crossing their hands on their little chests and bowing three times each in the prettiest gesture imaginable. The house-boy, who had introduced himself as something that sounded like Tuong, now awaited our pleasure, suggesting in a mixture of broken English and Spanish that we might like to take a stroll before supper, which, he said, would be ready at any hour we chose to indicate—ten o'clock? eleven? Spain again! and we some twelve thousand miles away from Europe!

*   *   *   *

We went out into the enchantment of the evening. Night had fallen, but the full moon now risen over the sea made it a place of light and shadows. We saw that our house stood isolated on a promontory, among dark pines and ghostly bushes of white frangipani whose heavy scent filled the air. Out on the water rode the fishing fleet, quite stationary without a breath of wind to fill their enormous sails, in the path of the moon glittering as though with a miraculous draught of silver fishes.

We wandered. Along the sea-front ran a road, an avenue of tamarinds, that strange tree whose roots coil overground like clusters of pale grey serpents. And this was the Orient too. But on the other side of the road, behind the trees, ran a row of houses which had nothing to do with the Orient at all; they were crumbling palaces of Spain, in their decay still distempered in pink and green and blue and ochre, ornamented with pilasters and cornices, balconies and balustrades, with slatted shutters to the windows, and here and there a swagger design of dolphins, foliage, or sea-horses, in flaking plaster, and over some doorways a lordly coat-of-arms.

All was silent; not a soul about. Narrow streets, the houses almost touching overhead, twisted steeply up the hill, lit by a single lantern stuck into a bracket; we might have been roaming through some village in Andalusia. But when we peered through a wrought-iron gate into a patio, we were startled to see a cheetah prowling up and down; it spat at us, and leapt against the bars.

* * * *

And then suddenly as we came to the end of the avenue of tamarinds, we found ourselves in a noisy, brightly-lit square, full of life; a market-place with all the usual booths piled with fruit, vegetables, flowers, baskets, straw hats the size of umbrellas, scarves, sandals, fish, poultry live and dead, some tethered goats, and the crowd moving about in their shifting of colour. Torches flared; a loud-speaker brayed unheeded above the cries of the vendors and the disputes of the purchasers. Laura put her hands over her ears, but I saw she was laughing.

* * * *

'Where *have* we got to?' I said, as we escaped.

'Shall we go back to our house now, or shall we go on for a little?' I liked hearing her say 'our house.'

'Let's go on—that is, if you're not tired.'

'How could I be tired? This evening will never happen again.'

*   *   *   *

We went on, and all was quiet once more, save for the distant uproar of the market, and even that had faded away when I stopped dead in the middle of a piece of waste ground.

'Look!' I whispered, for I was truly awed.

There, before us, on a high hill, stood the façade of a ruined church. We could see that it was only a façade, for the moonlight glinted sharply behind the tracery of the windows. We could see also that it was an example of the most flamboyant Spanish baroque, being extravagantly embellished by statues and carvings, including a complete galleon manned by a skeleton.

An immensely broad flight of steps led up to the portals, but we did not climb them. I think we both felt that this dead monument was best left to its own tragic dignity, under the Cross which still lifted its arms to the moon on the highest gable, repeated by the constellation of the Southern Cross in the sky. We could not behave as tourists in this place. Instead, we turned away, engulfing ourselves in a dark street, the *Calle de la iglesia*, which led us to an open square flanked on one side by a Buddhist temple. We entered the forecourt. The absolute stillness seemed the embodiment of Quietism, the renunciation of all strife and aggression. The wisdom of passivity. Not a leaf stirred. The air was

75

heavy with the incense-like scent of joss-sticks, whose tiny red tips punctured the darkness under the threads of their thin blue smoke standing unwaveringly straight.

Two vast yellow lanterns dimly lit the interior. On the steps in front of the altar, if that is what it should be called, knelt a Chinese woman with her child; she held its hands together by the wrists, and moved them up and down in a silent lesson of prayer. I cannot tell why this babyish gesture touched me so deeply. Perhaps it was the contrast between the wrecked Christian church and this evidence of continuity in Faith, so differently conceived but as necessary to the Chinese peasant as to the bygone intellectual Jesuit builders of this Spanish colony.

*　　　*　　　*　　　*

Next day, when we had rejoined our ship, I thought the Colonel eyed me with suspicion.

'Had a good trip?'

'Very, thanks.'

He said no more for the moment, but presently he returned obliquely to the subject. Laura had just passed us, walking round and round the deck.

'Charming woman, Mrs. Drysdale,' he said, with a nod in her direction.

'Charming, yes. You think so?'

'Know her at home?'

'Slightly.'

'Tell me something about her.'

I don't know what mischief seized me, but I said, 'She's the sort of woman who would never quack beside you in any wood.'

The poor Colonel looked terribly puzzled.

*   *   *   *

Having drawn a blank with me, he has been trying to improve upon his own acquaintance with Laura. The moment he sees her sitting by herself, even though she has a book open on her knee, he pulls up a chair and plumps himself down beside her. I was still so much under the sweet influence of the evening we had spent alone together that at first I scarcely noticed his intrusion. I, who had never felt any desire for domesticity, had curiously tasted its flavour in the hours when we sat over our supper and afterwards talked in what I could feel only to be a perfect communion. I had felt secure, almost satisfied. But now, when I see her smile up at him— the same smile with which she greets me—a strange pang of resentfulness shoots through me. I had flattered myself that she enjoyed my company; now I began to wonder whether she was all things to all men. A charming woman. . . . Wasn't it the function of charming women to make any man feel for the time being that he was the successful one-and-only?

'Don't you find the Colonel rather a bore?'

'Colonel Dalrymple? No, I think he's very nice. A simple soul. And so good-looking.'

'What makes you think him a simple soul?'

'Well, obviously. And so dependable. One could rely on him in a shipwreck.'

'Shipwrecks occur so seldom in a life-time. For ordinary purposes I prefer people to be amusing.'

*   *   *   *

I am disturbed by the tumult of my emotions when I see the Colonel hanging round Laura. Now that she has pointed it out I notice that he is certainly good-looking; I watch them as they pace the deck together, a handsome pair, he taller than she though she is tall for a woman, and both so slim and elegant. Also so unmistakably English. Well-bred English—and I a man of the people! I see myself as a rough terrier beside a greyhound. Has Laura been merely tolerating me all this time? I know she has a kind heart, for when I once asked her what quality she most esteemed, she replied without hesitation 'Compassion.'

She can keep her compassion for those not too proud to accept it.

Yet what right have I to scrutinise much less to criticise the way she chooses to pursue? It is natural that she should prefer the company of her social equals. All the same, I cannot help remembering the tone of her voice when we parted for the night on that happy evening; 'Goodnight, Laura,' I had said, and she replied, 'Goodnight, dear Edmund; sleep well.' Conventional words, but I swear there was affection, even some tenderness, in her accents and in the look she gave me. Perhaps, since then, I have unwittingly become too possessive in my thoughts, too prone to regard her as *my* friend, *my* Laura, to whom nobody else had any claim. I had been so determined to make no demands upon her nor to enlist her sympathy in any way; all I asked was that for these last few weeks I might uninterruptedly enjoy her presence and the delight of her companionship. It was a humble enough aspiration. Now I find myself frustrated . . . or do I exaggerate?

I must not allow myself to become sour. I must not say sarcastic things about that man, that healthy animal. I had thought of my love as a selfless thing, beautiful as a mountain and as useless; any small meanness would damage its purity. Let me preserve it intact to the last.

*   *   *   *

We get a lot of fun out of the rumours that rush round the ship, inflating as they go, like giant balloons until somebody comes along to prick them. We had a good one this morning, when we were, in fact, waiting for an unpunctual pilot.

'Vy are ve arrested?'

'Do you mean stopped?'

'Yes, stop. Vy is ve sheep stop?'

'They say there's a man overboard.'

'The Chief Officer . . .'

'Have you heard? The Chief Officer's gone overboard.'

'Sharks in these waters . . .'

'Have you heard? A shark got the Chief Officer

by the leg just as he was stepping on to the gangway.'

'No, pliss. Zat is not right. Ve vait because Viet Nam ambassador left bottom.'

'?'

'He means left behind.'

'Behind is bottom, yes? no? same?'

'Not quite the same, Herr Braun.'

*   *   *   *

How much one still has to learn, and how little time I have to learn it. A phrase came back to me, out of a letter from a love-sick boy: 'You know how sometimes one looks at the person one loves when they do not know one is looking, and all one's love wells up in one? Especially when they are asleep.'

No, I did not know. I remember smiling rather patronisingly at the ungrammatical effusion of my young friend. Most persons, I thought, sleep with their mouth open, so wide as to invite you to drop a bun into it; many, oh worst of human degradations, snore. Now I know better, for I have come upon Laura asleep. Her book had fallen from her hand; she lay relaxed, in an attitude of loose grace and innocence. All the strength of her usual reserve had ebbed away from her; her defences gone. I had a revelation of her vulnerability as though like an eavesdropper I had spied upon her, alone and in tears. It was not only the softness of her limbs that thus moved me, but the intimation of the private

80

being within the self-sufficient image. This was a woman I was looking at, not a woman of the world.

And as I looked down upon her, my heart overflowing, I lost myself in the dangerous speculation of the wealth she could give to the one she loved, the faithfulness, the solicitude, the gaiety, the comradeship, the tenderness, the passion. A Laura that I should never be allowed to know. Farewell, thou art too dear for my possessing. . . . All that I can carry away is the recollection of that brief moment when I perceived her—yes, perceived is the right word—as I might have gazed upon her in the starlight as she lay sleeping in my arms.

*   *   *   *

I must retain that vision, with all the protective gentleness it holds, for I observe with dismay an increasing bitterness creeping into my soul. Can love so change its character? I thought I had suppressed the temptation to make demolishing remarks about the Colonel, and God knows I had thought up enough of them, in the long hours of the wakeful night. Besides affording some relief to my spleen, it gave me considerable entertainment as a game, almost an intellectual exercise, for my butt was manifestly such a decent chap that it taxed all my ingenuity to make convincing fun of him. I should have been by far the easier prey, with my clumsy ways and stocky build; I could quite imagine him asking Laura, not necessarily with a sneer, 'Where's your highbrow friend this morning?' Even so, I fancy that he would come off worst, in a battle of sarcasm.

Yet what could I find to say? He is not easy to attack. I resort to childish jibes, as futile as a school-boy envious of a more successful boy, a school-hero. 'Oh yes,' I say, 'a glamorous type, no doubt, even to his name, Mervyn Dalrymple. How could one take seriously a man called Mervyn Dalrymple? It is pure Ouida, my dear Laura; a dream-name invented by a lady novelist. It suits him, too; he looks the part and plays up to it . . .' quite untrue, for he is the last man ever to play up to any part. He is genuine and unself-conscious through and through; and so modest that if he had the V.C., which perhaps he has, he would be at pains to conceal it.

If I were that way inclined, which I am *not*, I can imagine falling in love with him myself. How strange a twist, that such a notion should even cross my mind!

I must be going mad.

I must stop it; stop it; stop it.

*   *   *   *

Yet I can't stop it. I find myself indulging in something even more cruel: silent monologues with Laura herself, in which I destroy all the world she stands for, idle, self-indulgent, vain. 'Of what value are you and your like,' I would say, 'tinsel on a Christmas tree, witches' balls reflecting reality upside down, deluding men with implicit promises you never mean to fulfil? And what would be

82

their fulfilment, even should you decide to grant it? A night of illusory bliss! Get you, not to a nunnery but to a harem. Spend your days lying on a divan, eating sweets, getting fatter and fatter and discussing love-philtres and aphrodisiacs with your female rivals. You flattered yourself that I loved you, did you? no, it was only your body that I desired. Men's business is with other things than the dalliance of love.' So I continue, until in imagination I have the satisfaction of making her cry.

And then I meet her in the morning, and she greets me with her usual friendliness, and I recover my sanity and feel like a Judas, remembering the venomous things I have said to her, of which she is so innocently unaware.

*   *   *   *

I came away on this voyage with such different intentions in my mind. I had said to myself that 'as the fires die and desires decay, so the mind steals away and walks abroad to see the little images of beauty and pleasure, which it beholds in the falling stars and little glow-worms of the world.' My fires of ambition, such as they were, have died or been renounced, and all I hoped for was that I might capture some images of beauty and pleasure, so long obscured for me by the contrary life I had led. I knew that the wish for them had always been latent. Now it seems that even the last frailty of an immaculate love must suffer tarnish.

Therefore my soul melts, and my heart's dear treasure
Drops blood (the only beads) my words to measure:
O let this cup pass, if it be thy pleasure.
　　Was ever grief like mine?

　　　　*　　　*　　　*　　　*

I don't know how it came about that the conversation between us turned upon marriage. We were drifting on a placid sea, watching the sun in its slow descent towards the west. We had been talking, I think, about two friends of ours who had recently divorced, when Laura remarked that it was surprising how many people managed to make a success of so difficult an undertaking as marriage.

'Most people,' I said, 'would put it the other way round.'

'I wasn't thinking,' she said, 'of a sustained ecstasy throughout the years. But I do think it surprising that any union should survive the irritation of two separate personalities impinging upon one another. One or the other is usually top dog, and that must always be hard for the under dog to accept.'

'Some women like it—and the under dog is the woman, in ninety-five cases out of a hundred.'

'But consider the women who don't like it,' she said, looking at me very gravely. 'Should it not be possible for a man and a woman to share their lives on level terms, as two men might, or two women? Each going their own way, and coming together again, enriched by their differing experiences?'

I was wondering whether she was thinking of her own marriage, when she said unexpectedly,

'Tommy was killed in the war, you know, and I have been free for so long that perhaps I am not a very good judge.'

I did not quite know how to take this; I knew very little about Tommy Drysdale, except that he had been a good soldier who played cricket for his county. And Laura is not a person to encourage intimate questions.

'I never met your husband,' I said lamely.

'No, you wouldn't. Tommy didn't care for the sort of people that you and I like. You would have been amused by the kind of world that I frequented in those days. So worthy! Every thought in its right place. I used to call it the Send-a-frigate-school-and-show-these-dagoes-where-they-get-off.'

'Then why,' I couldn't help saying, 'with your views on independence in marriage, did you comply? You seem to agree with Montaigne, that marriage is a covenant having nothing free but the entrance, the continuance being forced and constrained.'

'I was a good deal younger then,' she said, rather sadly, I thought.

'Not that I wasn't fond of Tommy,' she resumed. 'I recognised all his good qualities, I admired his courage, I was even very much in love with him when we married. Only, I was far too young and inexperienced to realise how utterly unsuited we were. It took me a year to find out.'

This was the first time that I had ever heard Laura

speak of herself. I longed to ask her to go on, but was afraid of scaring her away.

'So you see,' she continued after a pause, 'why I have thought about marriage and come to my own conclusions. Tommy wouldn't have allowed me to go to a dinner-party without him, and as for having my own friends! . . . I did ask a young violinist to the house once, he played for us after dinner, hours and hours. And all Tommy said was that he needed a hair-cut.'

'Poor Laura.'

'Oh, I wasn't really to be pitied and I don't want you to think me disloyal—to Tommy's memory, I mean—only I was trying to analyse out loud what had made me so fiercely independent now. You see, I cannot abide the Mr. and Mrs. Noah attitude towards marriage; the animals went in two by two, forever stuck together with glue. I resent it as much for other people as I should for myself. It seems to me a degradation of individual dignity.'

'You see people very much as individuals, I think. I have noticed that.'

'I value personal liberty for everybody as much as you can value liberty for—shall I say the Press?'

I laughed.

'The Press is a thing of my past. I now prefer salt water to ink.'

'But you'll go back to it, won't you, Edmund? How would the British public get on without you to tell it what to think?'

'Never mind about the British public, I am more

interested in your views on matrimony. It is not a subject to which I have given much attention. Tell me your recipe for a workable marriage.'

She held up her hand and began ticking off the points.

'Mutual respect. Independence, as I have said, both as regards friends and movement. Separate bedrooms—no bedroom squalor. You know how a chance remark may stick and influence one's whole outlook? Once, when I was a young girl, I heard someone define it as hair-combings floating in a basin of soapy water and I've never forgotten. Separate sitting-rooms—if the house is large enough. Separate finances. I've come to the end of my fingers.'

'And what about community of interests?'

'Nice, but not essential. What *is* essential, is the same sense of values.'

'Meaning that one must be shocked, or otherwise, by the same things?'

'Exactly. And amused by the same things too.'

'And what about fidelity? Is the liberty of the spirit to extend to the liberty of the body?'

She hesitated.

'I can't prescribe. I would say it must depend on the other person. I feel sure that one should avoid giving pain; it is an elementary part of the bargain of marriage. After all, I did live up to that principle in a minor way; I never offended Tommy's conventional ideas because I knew it would hurt him, and short of breaking away altogether I knew that no compromise was possible.'

'How long could you have kept it up?'

She shrugged.

'I have often wondered. As one grows older and becomes more aware, one also becomes less inclined for self-immolation. Unless one has a saintly character, which I haven't. But in my case Fate intervened. Tommy was killed, and that solved any problem I might have been confronted with. Now have I scandalised you by my unwomanly theories?'

'You haven't scandalised me in the least. I can think of many men who would be the better for hearing them.'

'Then what are you grinning at?'

'At some of your assumptions, Laura dear. Separate bedrooms, separate sitting-rooms. In the cottage where I was born there were only two bedrooms and one living-room which was also the kitchen. If an uncle came to stay, I was turned out of my bedroom and slept on a truckle-bed on the landing. My bedroom was little more than a large cupboard anyhow.'

She looked a little embarrassed.

'I was thinking of the sort of people we both know,' she said. 'I think perhaps different laws may apply for . . . for people living as you describe. I think perhaps their acceptance is simpler than ours. The man is the wage-earner, the woman stays at home to cook, and mind the children. They are bound together by a necessity they never dream of questioning.'

'H'm. Very well, we will continue to consider only

the well-to-do. In all this discussion there is one element you have entirely left out: love.'

'Ah, love!' she said, a deeper note coming into her voice. It seemed to sink an octave. 'Well, if you want to know what I think about that I will tell you. He was a foolish cynic who said that great love occurred only two or three times in a century. There is nothing more lovely in life than the union of two people whose love for one another has grown through the years from the small acorn of passion into a great rooted tree. Surviving all vicissitudes, and rich with its manifold branches, every leaf holding its own significance. Is there not some passage in Homer about such a love being a joy to the people concerned and a source of irritation to their friends?'

'Something like that, but you have improved upon Homer. He was innocent of irony. For him, it was a *pleasure* to their friends. Your psychology is subtler than his.'

'I still maintain,' she said, 'that such a love can be achieved only by the practice of mutual respect and personal liberty. Look, I will show you something I have never shown anyone else. I read it somewhere once, I can't remember where, and copied it out and have got into the habit of using it as a book-marker. Read it.'

I read:

> Love one another, but make not a bond of love.
> Fill each other's cup but drink not from one cup.

Let there be spaces in your togetherness
And let the winds of heaven dance between you.

Sing and dance together and be joyous and let each one
    of you be alone,
Even as the strings of a lute are alone though they
    quiver with the same music.

Stand together, yet not too near together;
For the pillars of the temple stand apart
And the oak tree and the cypress grow not in each
    other's shadow.

* * * *

'Look,' she said as I returned the paper to her,
'the sun is nearly down, let us go and watch for our
green flash. The sky is clear, it should be good
tonight.'

The sky was indeed clear, of the palest blue with
a few little pink clouds floating; and as the earth
rolled over, the sun sank with the rapidity that
never failed to surprise me. It touched the horizon;
was cut in half; disappeared; and there came the
flash. Laura clapped her hands like a child.

'How could you compare it to jade? I said much
more truly that it was emerald.'

'If I remember rightly, you said call it green as
jealousy and be done with it.'

'And you replied that you had never known the
meaning of jealousy.'

'Did I? Fancy that!'

* * * *

90

They dance on deck after dinner, under strings of coloured lights that quiver slightly with the vibration of the ship. I can't dance; never could; too uncouth, I suppose. The eager Englishwoman skittishly tried to coax me, seeing her chance in one of those turns when the women instead of the men select their partners. 'Oh, come now, Mr. Carr, don't be so coy.' Grrrh!

Laura, who is much in demand, dances mostly with the Colonel. He comes to claim her as though it were a foregone conclusion that she would accept. She rises, and melts into his arms as though they were made for one another. I go away to the bar and order myself a glass of beer.

*   *   *   *

Children take naturally to Laura. She never appears to pay any attention to them, but I have watched them stealing nearer and nearer to her as she sits reading on deck, like small animals allured by some appetising scent. Then at last she will resignedly lay down her book, and look round the circle of little faces, and say, 'Well, what now?' And then they will come closer, and the boldest will scramble on to her lap, and she will let them play with the numerous charms she wears on a bangle round her wrist. I have often glanced sideways at those charms myself, wondering whether each one represented the gift of some lover. Unlike me, the children never enquire as to their origin; they are content to take them at their face value. 'What's that, Mrs. D'ysdale?' and then with infinite patience Laura tells them a story about each. They never seem to tire of this game; children can bear any amount of repetition, and any variation is instantly resented. 'You didn't say it like that last time, Mrs. D'ysdale; tell it the same as you did before.' 'Oh Robert, how stupid of me to make a mistake. I'll get it right this time. You see, Robert, once upon a time this little elephant was a real big live elephant, and he worked so hard in the jungle carrying tree-trunks in his own trunk (squeals of laughter at the joke) that some nice kind magician said he deserved a rest, so he turned him into this tiny elephant for me to wear on my bracelet.'

'And what's this, Mrs. D'ysdale?'

'Well, that's a little porpoise. He got tired of living in the sea, so he asked his own magician if he could come on a ship instead, and get carried to countries he had never seen. His name is Delfino.'

'Delfino! What a funny name.'

'I've been to a restaurant called Delfino, in Naples,' said a superior eight-year-old, but they did not want to hear about that.

'Mrs. D'ysdale, tell about this.'

'Oh, that's a coin, a gold coin. Can you see, it has got the head of King Charles the First on it. Poor King Charles, they cut his head off.'

'Is that why you have got his head on your bracelet?'

'Is it *reel* gold?'

'Was he a naughty King?'

92

'Silly, of course he was. I've learnt about him in the history books. Else they wouldn't have cut his head off.'

'What's this, please?'

'That,' said Laura, 'is a thing called the Cross of the Liberation.'

'Why?'

But I never heard what reason Laura invented to explain the Cross of the Liberation, for I went away wondering what on earth she had done to earn it.

*　　　*　　　*　　　*

There is a little spastic boy to whom she devotes herself daily, reading to him, showing him pictures in illustrated magazines, letting him play with her repeater watch and its tinkling chimes. He is in a wheeled chair, his legs in irons, but can just stagger grotesquely with the help of a hand. Tall Laura and this hobbling dwarf go for painstaking walks when the ship is steady enough; she encourages him, although she knows full well that he will never regain the use of his limbs. But she is teaching him to draw, for his hands and arms are unaffected and he displays a certain talent which she thinks might be developed. 'Why, Peter,' she says, 'one day you may become a famous architect and build beautiful houses for people to live in.' Then he perseveres by himself, and produces designs which he shows her with pride and some anxiety next day.

His mother cannot get over the way in which Laura has won his adoration.

93

'Ever since his illness, when he got like that a year ago,' she told me, 'he would scarcely speak to anybody but us—as though he were ashamed, you know, of not being like other boys—sullen, wouldn't take any interest in anything. I really thought some spring was broken inside him. But Mrs. Drysdale seems to have put fresh life into him. I only hope he doesn't relapse when he gets away from her. We live in London, and she says she will come and see him. Do you think she will?'

'If she says so, I am quite sure she will.'

Selfishly, I am always aware of a pang when I hear people making plans for a future I shall not see.

How small-minded one is.

*   *   *   *

Laura is full of indignation.

'The injustice of it!' she says. 'That innocent child, his life ruined! Why, Edmund? One has only one life. What has he done to deserve this?'

'Miss Corcoran would say he is expiating the sins of a former existence.'

'Damn Miss Corcoran. How much I hate, and how little I understand, pain and frustration of that sort. Of any sort, indeed. It seems to me on a par with evil—ugly, unnecessary, cruel.'

'That dear old priest over there would tell you that God sent it as a trial for our benefit. God is love, God is just, God is merciful. Can you see any logical justification for such beliefs? Any evidence to support them? All the evidence goes against them. Loving kindness, justice, and mercy! Good God! Why does one say Good God! as an exclamation? One might equally say Bad God, or Indifferent God, or just merely God, or indeed Od, which would perhaps be the best form of address to our incomprehensible deity.'

'Oh do shut up, Edmund, and stop bewildering me with your jokes. I never intended this to turn into a theological discussion. Your dear old priest over there has to get out of the difficulty somehow. And I daresay we have all merited chastisement by the time we reach middle-age. But not a child! Now supposing you or I, Edmund, were suddenly to find ourselves smitten, we could say to ourselves that we had had our life, and enjoyed it, and made some use of it, and were ready to pay for any ill-doing. I should try to make that my philosophy, without rebellion. I don't say that I should succeed.'

She little knows the irony of such words, addressed to me. They are salutary, none the less. I have had my life, and enjoyed it, and have made some use of it, and ought not to grudge seeing the last prize denied me.

'How should we take it?' she went on. 'Something unseen, gnawing at one. The certainty of a shortened life. Would one's entire outlook be altered? Would one's standard of values change? Would one tell anybody?'

'I don't think one would tell anybody,' I said. 'One would creep away into a corner by oneself, and wait.'

95

'I believe I should prefer that to the fate of that wretched child,' she said. 'He has all his years before him, one long refusal of everything that normality should give. At least he is spared pain. Pain is such a terrible thing, Edmund; I have seen so much of it, and I can't tell you what I feel about it. I am really not sane on the subject,' she said with a smile.

'You mean the war? You nursed?'

'Part of the time.'

'In England?'

'Yes, and in France. Now I must go and change for dinner.'

She was evidently unwilling to say more, and although I was full of curiosity I did not like to press her.

* * * *

I dare not ask her whether she ever had any children of her own, for fear of some tragedy in the background—she may have lost one in infancy, and her interest in the little ailing boy may not be entirely objective; or they may have grown up unsatisfactory and be too painful a subject to mention. Say she is forty now, and married at eighteen, she could easily have an adult son or daughter. My mind flies to all kinds of possibilities: a boy expelled from school, a girl making a runaway match with a scamp. . . . Somehow, despite her 'way' with children, I cannot see her as a mother. She is not the maternal woman; too cerebral perhaps; but the perfect friend and lover.

* * * *

I also, like the little boy, am fortunate in that this disease which I know must be eating into me causes me no suffering, so that for long hours together I forget all about it. Waking in the morning, I come slowly to my senses with the dim awareness of something unpleasant hanging over me, as on days when one has some tedious duty to perform, and then remembrance returns. 'Of course. I am due to die.'

It is a curious feeling. I wonder sometimes whether all those who wait upon the shore of death accept the fact with such indifference as I? Death, it has been said, (though not, I think, by Francis Bacon) 'arrives graciously only to those who sit in darkness, or lie heavily burthened with grief and irons; to the poor Christian that sits bound in the galley; to despairful widows, pensive prisoners, and deposed kings; to them whose fortune runs back and whose spirits mutiny—with such Death is a redeemer, and the grave a place for retiredness and rest.'

I am certainly neither a despairful widow nor a pensive prisoner nor a deposed King, nor do I regard Death as a redeemer since I enjoy life and have no wish to retire from it, and somehow try as I may I cannot bring myself to envisage my end as imminent. After all, most people as they approach their end, unless it comes suddenly and with violence, have their faculties so greatly impaired by illness or extreme old age that they are no longer capable of analysis or sensation. I, on the contrary, retain all my faculties and am in what delusively appears to be normal physical health. I suppose the fact is that subconsciously we shove the ultimate truth aside. How much better to accept it in all its simplicity.

*   *   *   *

Take away but the pomps of death, the disguises and solemn bugbears, the tinsel and the actings by candlelight, and proper and fantastic ceremonies, the minstrels and the noise-makers, the women and the weepers, the swoonings and the shriekings, the nurses and the physicians, the dark room and the ministers, the kindred and the watchers; and then to die is easy, ready, and quitted from its troublesome circumstances. It is the same harmless thing that a poor shepherd suffered yesterday, or a maid-servant today.

*   *   *   *

Without wishing to make excuses for myself, I daresay that my condition heightens my susceptibilities and strips me of several skins. Otherwise I cannot explain the insane impulses which overwhelm me. A reasonably honourable man as a rule, I now find myself a prey to temptations which previously would never have entered my head and which, I confess, appal me. For instance, Laura, meeting me in the passage on my way to the purser's office, asked me to drop her letters into the mail-box as I passed it. Before I knew what I was doing I found myself examining the addresses to discover to whom she had been writing. Not a great crime in itself, perhaps, but mean, mean! They were all to people of whom I had never heard, her private life in which I had no part. I was horrified by the rage which made

98

me dizzy, and even more horrified by the whisper suggesting that I might steam them open and learn the worst or find relief.

'Ralph Ramsay Esq., Iron Ashton Manor, Ashton, Somerset.' Who could that be? Or Sir Paul Livingstone, Bart.? The others I dismissed, for they were clearly business letters. I must take a great pull on myself; this will never do.

*　　　*　　　*　　　*

If ever there was a thing I deprecated it was meanness, petty suspicion, reluctance to give the benefit of the doubt, the desire to score off others, the search for unworthy motives, cruelty, spite. I had seen enough of it all, both in my boyhood and in my profession. I had tried to suppose that it all made up the fascination of human nature—so small and vile on the one hand, so capable of surprising nobility and charity on the other. It is hard that an uncontrollable emotion should now force me down into the very trough I had deliberately shunned.

*　　　*　　　*　　　*

She receives letters too; I have seen a steward bringing them to her.

'No letters for poor Edmund?' she said, laying hers aside.

'Poor Edmund doesn't want any. He has sloughed his old skin, like a snake.'

It is quite true. Relations I have none, and no wish to hear from my friends; I did leave a couple of addresses with my Editor, but only under coercion, and when he wrote asking me to clear up some point which had provoked correspondence in his columns I found that I had to wrench my mind round before I could take even a perfunctory interest in his enquiry. It was the sort of thing which in the old days would have roused me to rattling off pages of diatribe.

Why can I not achieve this pitch of indifference to everything else?

*   *   *   *

I do make an occasional effort, telling myself that this canker of the mind, this frightening obsession of jealousy is without foundation, but every time something happens to frustrate my best intentions. This time I exaggerate it to the proportions of a major infliction. The married couple and their daughter have disembarked, and their place at Laura's table has been taken by another married couple and, of all people, the Colonel. So now I have to watch them talking and laughing together through a long meal twice a day; I note how swiftly he picks up her napkin when she drops it, pours out wine for her, holds his lighter to her cigarette. The merrier they are, the gloomier grow I, asking myself endlessly whether this change in the seating is just a chance arrangement of the head steward's, or whether it has taken place through complicity. Did she tell Dalrymple that her former companions were leaving and suggest that he should ask for a transfer? That would mean that she prefers his company to mine. Or did he find it out for himself, and seize the opportunity to move? If so, why could I not have profited by a similar prescience? My usual incompetence; I was always a square wheel. Whichever way I look at it, I feel hurt and thwarted, and the more convinced I become of their collusion.

> I that was once the music of these valleys,
> So darkened am, that all my day is evening,
> Heart-broken so, that molehills seem high mountains.

*   *   *   *

But are they molehills? It is dreadful how I twist the slightest thing into a confirmation of suspicions I do not want confirmed. I remember stray remarks of Laura's and construe them under the glare of a different light. There had been the young steward who brings the coffee after dinner; had I noticed him, she asked?

'I can't say I have,' I said. 'Unlike some of our friends at home, I don't take any particular notice of young men. What about him?'

'Well, look how graceful he is; he might be a dancer. From Bali. So sinuous. Look how he weaves between the tables. And he has a crooked smile, which is very attractive, and one pointed ear like a faun. A dangerous person to have about.'

At the time I thought she had spoken flippantly, and paid little heed, but now I am not so sure. What lies under her cool exterior? Was her appreciation

101

of this boy's wry beauty indicative of her own sensuality? One has often been surprised by the discovery of hidden things going on for years in lives of the highest repute—why not in hers? She is still young, she is attractive God knows, she is free—what is to prevent her from indulging herself in the most fleeting caprice? She is deep and secretive; one would never know.

From here is but a step to remembering her comment on Dalrymple's good looks, and he a man of her own class. Yes, she is moved by the handsome male, no doubt about it. She can become eloquent over black dock-hands, naked to the waist.

'Look, Edmund, what a magnificent torso, what shoulders, what muscles! polished like metal, pure sculpture. How a black skin enhances colour—see how his red loin-cloth shows up redder than it would on a white man. Look at their natural carriage, so straight and erect, and their springing walk—like athletes.'

I wish I could believe her observations to be wholly aesthetic, but the touch of sex is in it. Or so my disordered mind persuades me to surmise. And why not, I say to myself, ashamed of my unworthy fancies? She is very much a woman, and her affinity is man. Her very frankness should perhaps be disarming: people are careful not to betray that which they have reason to conceal. It is not exactly that I suspect her of promiscuity; only that I record her susceptibility, and, knowing her distaste for any hypocritical convention, deduce that a sufficiently powerful inclination would lead her to seek its natural term. Not the little steward, not a darkie— unless she is more of an experimentalist than I give her credit for—but Dalrymple . . . ah, that's another matter.

I look at him, I look at her, and I wonder.

*　　　*　　　*　　　*

A most unfortunate incident has not improved the situation. Laura and I had gone ashore, and despite the blazing heat decided to walk the mile that separated the quay from the native market, a dreary dusty road, mercifully shaded by an avenue of tired-looking trees but with little else to recommend it. Some mangy dogs growled at us as we went past, too languid to get up; a child followed us, a miserable morsel, whining for alms; it had no hands, and kept thrusting its pitiful stumps forward for our notice. I hoped Laura did not know what I knew, that the parents of these children cut off their hands at birth to make more effective beggars of them. Truly, a delightful world!

Laura has a passion for native markets, not shared by me, but I would do anything to please her. She likes the colour and the jostle and the strange medley of types, she likes the booths hung with pots and baskets and fluttering stuffs (made in Manchester), and I suspect she likes the underlying violence which might flare out in a brawl at any moment. Certainly there was noise enough as we

103

approached the square, the usual din of shouts mingled with the bleating of goats, and somewhere a drum monotonously beating, and a gramophone grinding out a wail in a minor key. Not much relishing this horde of wild-looking people, I noticed that there were no Europeans amongst them, a fact which made me uneasily apprehensive that they might resent our presence, but Laura said only that these must be tribes come down from the hills for a rare market day and that we must go and have a look at them at close quarters as we were never likely to have such an opportunity again.

I was hoping not, when to my relief I saw a small brown policeman in khaki shorts sauntering towards us. He carried a rifle slung across his shoulder and a revolver protruded from his belt, but in spite of this armoury he did not look to me much of a match against an angry crowd. He addressed some unintelligible remarks to us, in which I could distinguish only the word No several times repeated, accompanied by an unmistakably negative wagging of the hand.

'Look here,' I said, 'he doesn't want us to go any further.'

'Oh, nonsense,' said Laura, 'I'm not going back now. They make a lot of noise, but nothing ever comes of it. It's not as though we were going to take photographs of a religious procession.'

'Please, Laura.'

'If you won't come with me, I shall go by myself.'

I couldn't detain her by force and had no choice

but to follow her into that seething macaw-coloured clangorous mob. The instant the booth-keepers observed her, they were round her, scenting foreign money, competing with one another, 'This way, lady, this way.' That was a harmless nuisance, common to all souks and bazaars, but what I did not like was the dark glances cast upon us by countless eyes. These were rough men; how rough, I did not care to speculate. What if one of them were to lay hands on Laura and hustle her from their exclusive site? What would I do then? If I were to intervene, we should have the whole rabble of them upon us. Even the little policeman, with his meagre authority, had remained strolling his beat at a distance; he had given his warning, in duty bound, and if the strangers chose to disregard it so much the worse for them.

All I could pray was that some internal diversion should arise to distract their attention from ourselves, some squabble on the grand scale, ending in blows and bodies rolling on the floor, while everybody rushed up to take part. And this is indeed what happened. An enormous negress, incongruously swathed in pale pink muslin, entered into some argument with a group of men; lost her temper; struck one of them on the nose with a fist the size of a boxing-glove; blood poured; partisans, both men and women, joined in; I saw the flash of knives, heard yells as though some ancient feud were being avenged. I seized Laura by the arm.

'Here, let's get out of this.'

The little policeman, as we passed him, grinned.

*   *   *   *

Our walk back to the quay was not enjoyable. Having been frightened, I was angry with Laura, and said,

'That's the first time I have ever known you to be tiresome.'

She seemed quite unruffled.

'It was interesting, didn't you think? Like children in a sudden quarrel. By now they are probably all good friends again. I expect it happens several times a day.'

'Perhaps you think that is the way to live?'

'Well, I have often wanted to box somebody's ears—haven't you?'

'Yes, yours, just now.'

'You're cross with me, Edmund.'

'You were stupidly reckless. I don't admire that sort of pluck. I suppose it was your disregard of danger that won you the Croix de la Libération?'

She looked startled.

'How did you know I had the Croix de la Libération?'

'Never mind.'

*   *   *   *

That would have been the end of it, but in the evening the Colonel came up to me.

'Nasty business, that might have been.'

106

How had he heard about it? I felt sure Laura would not have told him. But in ship-life news travels rapidly.

'You never can tell, you know,' he continued, 'when these fellows will turn nasty. Very unpleasant for a woman. Blood, and all that. Very unpleasant for Mrs. Drysdale.'

I realised then that he was an indignant man, and that did not make me like him any the better.

'I've lived a lot among natives in my time,' he went on, 'and I know one shouldn't go barging in amongst them unnecessarily in their own compounds. They have their own ways of settling their differences, and our best plan is to keep clear. So long as they don't interfere with us, of course, or get too much out of hand. But if you go barging in you're just asking for trouble. If you don't mind my saying so, you should never have taken Mrs. Drysdale in amongst that riff-raff.'

'I do mind your saying so. I don't see what business it is of yours. I have known Mrs. Drysdale a great deal longer than you have. And in any case, it was she who took me, not I who took her.'

'Well!' he began, explosively, 'if you haven't the guts to stop a woman, there's no more to be said. I'm glad only that she got off so lightly.'

I wished I were like that uncivilised negress and could crash my fist into his damned handsome face. My anger was not diminished by the knowledge that he was right: I should have stopped her. If anything had happened to her I should never have

107

forgiven myself. This did not prevent me from raging off to find her.

'Your precious Colonel has taken upon himself to read me a lecture.'

'I thought he would. I've had one too.'

'Damned impudence.'

'Yes, so I thought,' said Laura, which mollified me. 'What did you say?'

'Not a quarter of what I should like to have said. I told him to mind his own business, and that I'd known you a great deal longer than he had.'

'He meant well, I've no doubt.'

'He can keep his good intentions to himself in the future.'

'Now you are not going to scowl and be disagreeable to him, Edmund, are you? It will make things so awkward. Here we are all three on this ship and although you may not like him you can't get away from him.'

'I never said I didn't like him. I do like him. I wish I could help liking him. I only said it was damned impudence to take me to task, and so it is. I'm not a child.'

'No, but I was afraid you might behave like one.'

She had soothed me, partly by her calm and partly by her implication that she and I were confederates. We had both been scolded, equally. My one comfort in the whole silly affair is that Laura attributes my annoyance to my natural resentment at being lectured by another man, not even a friend, and never assumes that it might have anything to do with my feelings towards herself. The intolerable thought of another man setting himself up in any way as her guardian! I try to persuade myself that perhaps he doesn't; that perhaps it is just inherent in his character to watch over the safety of any woman; that perhaps he was honestly trying to give me the benefit of his advice. 'Never trust a white woman among niggers, my dear chap'—I could hear him saying it. This was in my better moods, but even so I knew well that I sought to delude myself: his suppressed anger had been personal, not objective.

*   *   *   *

They seem to have made it up and to be as good friends as ever. They pace the decks, laugh at the porpoises, play deck-quoits, and dance together. Miss Corcoran gazes after them enraptured, investing them with all the romance she has missed.

'I often think it so sad, don't you, Mr. Carr,' she says, 'that these ship-board friendships usually come to an end with the voyage. And yet I don't know,' she added more hopefully, 'I knew a very nice couple once, Braithwaite their name was, Mr. and Mrs. Braithwaite, they live at Godalming, near my sister—you know, the sister I was telling you about, the one who had such a bad attack of shingles, oh dear, oh dear, she *was* poorly—well, this Mr. and Mrs. Braithwaite had met, just like Mrs. Drysdale and Colonel Dalrymple if I may say so, on the old Rajputana going out to Bombay—he was in the

Indian Civil—ah, those were good days, weren't they, Mr. Carr, before we gave up India—such a mistake, I always thought—and look at them now, happily married in a dear little house and three lovely children. Grown up, of course, by now, and doing so well. Not that Mr. and Mrs. Braithwaite were anything like so good-looking as Mrs. Drysdale and the Colonel; oh, by no means. Poor Mrs. Braithwaite, she was always worrying about her figure, and he did go bald very young. But just look at those two, Mr. Carr: wouldn't they make a lovely match?'

'I should never have taken you for a match-maker, Miss Corcoran.'

'No? Well, isn't that funny? Just the contrary of what my sister always says, not the one who lives at Godalming, the one who lives in London. Such a dear little upper part she has, in Warwick Square; I wish you could see it. "Emily," she says, "you're a born match-maker, you ought to set up a matrimonial agency." Rather unkind, I think, don't you? But I'm sure you must agree about the Colonel and Mrs. Drysdale. A widow, I believe, isn't she?'

'So I have been given to understand.'

'I don't know about the Colonel. He may have left a wife in England, for all I know. I always think it so unfair on legal documents, where a woman has to put married, widow or spinster, so that you know at once where you are, whereas a man is just himself. Not on your passport, though, you don't, so in any case it wouldn't be any good getting a peep

110

at his. So many foreign men wear a wedding ring, don't they? I don't think I quite like that—it looks rather effeminate, I always think, a ring on a man's hand. Except for a signet ring on the little finger, of course. That is quite manly, and rather nice. But it's convenient, no doubt about it.'

'Even if you can't marry off Mrs. Drysdale to the Colonel, Miss Corcoran, there are other paths to romance outside marriage.'

Miss Corcoran was as shocked as I hoped she would be.

'Oh, Mr. Carr! how can you say such dreadful things? I'm sure neither Mrs. Drysdale nor the Colonel would ever. . . . Of course, we all know what men are. But not Mrs. Drysdale—oh no, *not* Mrs. Drysdale.'

*   *   *   *

All the same, I met Dalrymple coming out of Laura's cabin one evening between tea and dinner.

'Don't look so surprised. I was lending him a book.'

'Indeed?' I said before I could stop myself. 'I didn't know he could read.'

From the look she gave me, I fear I may have given myself away.

*   *   *   *

That is the last thing I want to do. When one has nothing to hope for, it is unpardonable selfishness to trouble the peace of other people, and if I truly loved Laura according to my ideals my last legacy

111

to her would be a wish for her happiness. I fall short. I try so hard to be reasonable, scoffing at my own imaginings, telling myself that there is nothing in it, not even the ghost of a flirtation—Laura is no flirt—but then I do know that she finds the man attractive and he for his part indubitably finds her very attractive indeed. The truth is, that I wanted her to myself for the short time left to me, and I hate him for spoiling that last poor boon I had asked of life. I suppose it is their insouciant health that I envy, and their expectation of many years to come; we are not competing on a fair basis. And what riles me in particular is the knowledge that there is nothing whatsoever in common between them; Laura would find the Colonel every whit as domineeringly male as Tommy Drysdale. She is quite sensible enough probably to see it already. Therefore, I argue miserably, that what draws them together is a purely animal accord, needing no complement of speech; a force of Nature.

What will it matter to me, after I am gone?

*   *   *   *

Alas poor silly man, thou hast but too, too many necessary and unavoidable incommodities, without increasing them by thine own invention, and art sufficiently wretched of condition without any art; thou aboundest in real and essential deformities, and needest not forge any by imagination.

*   *   *   *

I sometimes feel that this ship is wayward, having

no settled course but wandering where the fancy takes her, a theory which fits in exactly with my mood. My life hitherto has been too predictable; now that it has suddenly turned upside down I like to imagine a partner in caprice. How much I wish that I had travelled more, as a young man, gone on some exploring expedition, penetrated to places where no white man had ever stood before. The lure of affairs was too strong upon me, and I never gave travel a thought, which is odd, because as a boy I used to be fascinated by the big globe in our classroom, and used to creep back when the others were out in the playground, and put my finger on the remotest spot I could find, probably, had I but known it, in the middle of some Asian salt-desert—and whisper to myself 'I should like to be *there*.' I thought I had outgrown all such inklings of adventure, ludicrous enough in me who am neither courageous nor resourceful. At least I may say that I have reached middle-age without becoming blasé; although I may only be carried in comfort to civilised harbours my enjoyment is all the keener for never having left my native shores. I would not confess it even to Laura, but I am still capable of the same astonishment as 'the child that sees its first black man.'

* * * *

I have been annoyingly disconcerted: the Colonel has apologised. He came up to me with I must admit a disarming simplicity and said he hoped I would forget the words he ought not to have spoken.

'Of course it was none of my business, but long years of training, you know.... Got the better of me.'

I hope my acknowledgement was not too ungracious.

So now we play Bridge together in apparent amity. I must grant him a certain generosity, for few people find it easy to say that they are sorry, but perversely I grudge having to recognise any virtue in him. I wonder whether Laura put him up to it? I shan't ask her, in case she knows nothing about it. Far be it from me to advance him in her good opinion.

Mean! mean again.

*   *   *   *

I did however say to her that if she could lend books to the Colonel she might lend one to me too.

'I know I brought a whole crate on board, but other people's books always look so much more interesting than one's own.' The platitude would serve as a pretext.

The truth is that I wanted to see where she lived. I wanted to be able to visualise her brushing her hair at the dressing-table, moving amongst her possessions, lying in bed reading at night. All that I knew of her at home was her London drawing-room; I craved for a glimpse of something more intimate. It was probable that her cabin would be a replica of my own—those strange little impersonal boxes, clean as a convent cell, which become one's refuge for weeks and then are left stripped for another occupant. Round porthole, narrow bed, dressing-table with mirror, a stool, wardrobe, shelves, creamy washable walls, rubberoid on the floor, washing-place opening off behind a waterproof curtain. It would be exactly the same.

It was not the same at all. Laura had been at pains to prettify it, and the result was more like a room than a cabin. She had spread coloured silks over the bed and table; the pillowcases were rosy and frilly; she had abolished the ship's hideous ashtrays—I should never have noticed they were hideous if she hadn't once pointed it out to me—and had replaced them by some pottery she had bought in one of her precious markets; her books were aligned on a shelf—I had thrust all mine into a drawer—she had propped up some reproductions of Redouté's roses and a Chinese drawing of a very spirited horse. There were flowers, orchids, lilies, gardenias; had she bought them for herself, or had the Colonel provided them? I noted also some small ornaments, a crystal hawk, an amber Buddha, a white jade camel. No photographs, to my relief, except one of a Saluki dog stuck into the mirror.

'What do you do about all these things when it's rough?' I asked, unwilling to betray how moved I was by this evidence of her home-making instinct. A nesting-bird . . .

'I have to put them away, of course.'

'And what's that door?' I asked, pointing to a door

115

beside the porthole, for it had no counterpart in my own cabin.

'Ah, that's my great joy.' She opened it, and a swirl of hot air from outside rushed in. At once the mirror became misty with condensation, and I saw Laura and myself in it, as ghostly as the circumstances of our relationship. Another instant, and great tears would have started to trickle down. 'Shut it quickly behind you,' she said, 'or everything will begin to drip.'

I followed her out. We were on a little private balcony, furnished only by a bamboo chair and a tin table, entirely shut in from either side and from above. It overhung the sea, so much closer than our usual resort, the rails on the upper deck, that one had a sense of being one with the ship cleaving the waters.

'There are only four cabins with these balconies,' she said; 'two each side, or should I say two to port and two to starboard. I never know which is which. I was extravagant, and I don't regret it. You can't imagine how delicious it is, after a hot day, to stand out here in the evening and feel the breeze stroking one's skin.'

I could imagine it very well; I felt sure, although she had not said so, that she stood naked under that soft caress.

'So this is where you disappear to by the hour.'

We watched the dark sea in silence, the white marbling touched into life by the lights of the ship. Not for the first time I thought how easy it would be to end it all by slipping overboard in the night.

'It makes one want to throw oneself in, doesn't it?' she said unexpectedly. 'Like the impulse to jump from a high tower.'

'With the difference that if one jumped from a high tower one would land in a nasty mess, whereas here one would just glide down and down into blackness and be washed peacefully to and fro until one was eaten by fishes.'

'It would be extraordinarily cleansing,' she said. 'A sort of rebirth in death. Have you ever wished, Edmund, not that you could be reborn and have your life all over again only different, but that you could reverse your whole outlook and existence half-way through—I suppose that both you and I are half-way through or thereabouts—I'm forty, and I suppose I might live to eighty.'

'I'm fifty,' I said, 'and I very much doubt if I shall live to be a hundred.'

'Nor want to. Have you ever noticed, though, how few people would like to go back to being, say, twenty? If you ask them, they try to evade and say yes if they could take their present experience back with them. Others say no, not on any account. It makes one think that the average life must be remarkably unsatisfactory. Which would you say?'

'I've had a good life on the whole. It was a bit of a struggle at first, my people were very poor, and the village school isn't the best start for an education.

117

No Eton and Oxford for me.' I knew the Colonel had been to both.

'But you got scholarships, Edmund, I know you did.'

'Yes—to a grammar school and then to a red-brick University. It wasn't so easy in those days, over thirty years ago, and I hated having to ask my parents for financial help. I used to make a bit myself by writing for provincial newspapers.'

What I did not tell her was that these crabbed beginnings had left me with a sense of inferiority and an ignoble envy which I tried very hard to suppress.

'And then you came to London, I suppose?'

I saw that she was leading me tactfully on.

'I got a job as a sort of bottle-washer to a sub-sub-editor.'

'And what happened then?'

She was overcoming my reluctance.

'He fell ill, and I was made to act as his under-study. That was great fun,' I said. 'I saw my chance and took it. I brightened up his page, which wasn't difficult, so much that it quite frightened the people at the top.'

'And then?'

'Well, luckily for me, he died and I was kept on in his job. So you see I have nothing to complain of. Fate has been very kind to me.'

'Um. People largely make their own Fate.'

*   *   *   *

This conversation could perhaps scarcely be called very intimate—it was no more than I would have said to anyone who took the trouble to question me, and I daresay I had told her nothing she did not more or less know already. No. It was the vision of her cabin that left an impression on me. Archaeologists have a term, 'the small art,' as opposed to the major achievements of primitive man in the great cave paintings. Laura might not carve exquisite handles out of reindeer antlers nor trace patterns in the malleable clay of a bowl, but in this small art of her own she had found expression. It was a revelation to me of something I had missed. Great literature and great music had always been my solace, but the minor graces of life I had passed blindly by, too much concerned with public affairs, too passionately interested in permanent problems, too desirous of using such influence as I possessed. For this reason I had always preferred the company of men, and had often sighed as I put on my dinner-jacket to dine sitting between two pretty women, knowing that in their wish to flatter me they would try to draw me out, to get me to talk shop, and next day would repeat—all wrong—any response I had been so unguarded as to make. 'Oh, but, darling, Edmund Carr told me last night that he knew for certain . . .'

I looked back now on my preoccupied masculine life, absorbing but graceless; on my uncomely rooms, my ink-stained table, my shabby leather arm-chair, my rows of Hansard all toppling over,

119

my grimy curtains, and the waste-paper basket that never seemed to get emptied. The one Medici print, survival of my undergraduate days: van Gogh's sunflowers, hanging from a nail, invariably crooked. Sometimes a colleague would walk back with me, and then I would get out a siphon and the whiskey and we would sit talking, arguing, while the fog of smoke thickened and the fog of London obscured the stars outside.

Some of the women with whom I had transitory affairs insisted on coming to see where and how I lived and usually wanted to make me 'more comfortable.' They meant well, little knowing how much I resented interference and how little I relished being managed.

I begin to wonder now what transformation Laura would have worked, and to imagine what it would have been like to return to her of an evening, gently welcomed, never questioned, subtly cherished. I know without her telling me that she would have respected my liberty even as I should have respected hers. Such dreams beguile many an hour, until I build up so detailed a picture of an existence intolerable in its sweetness that it almost takes the place of something which had never been and in this world could never be . . . I smile to myself as I reflect on her surprise and confusion could she but read my thoughts.

* * * *

Sometimes the temptation comes over me to tell

her the whole truth. What harm could it do? She would know that I could ask nothing of her and that within a very short time she would be relieved of a presence which might have become irksome to her. But no: I refuse, even for a few days, to become a living reproach. She could no longer live on easy terms with a man whom she knew to be dying, a man who hopelessly loved her. This temptation should never come near me; I am appalled at my own weakness. I can turn to no outward help; my silence depends on my own strength, and at moments I feel that I have none.

I must leave her to others.

*   *   *   *

Who so list to hunt, I know where is an hind,
But as for me, alas, I may no more.
The vain travail hath wearied me so sore
I am of them that farthest come behind.
Yet may I by no means my wearied mind
Draw from the Deer, but as she fleeth afore
Fainting I follow. I leave off therefore,
Since in a net I seek to hold the wind.

*   *   *   *

Laura has always treated me with friendliness; in London she used to seem pleased to see me, and on board, until the intrusion of the unwanted third, I was her constant companion. Even with him hanging around, she seems welcoming when I find her alone, invites me to sit beside her, and never lets her glance stray over my shoulder to see if he is any-

121

where about. It may be her good manners. It may also be my heightened sensibility that sometimes makes me imagine an increased kindliness in her eyes, a caress in her voice, and an encouragement to talk about anything connected with myself. I find that my spirits rise or droop in the most unaccustomed way: half an hour spent with her, and I am almost content; then I see her with the Colonel, and the cloak of despond blackly descends again upon me.

These varying uncontrollable moods so greatly afflicting me are like the sea which I have grown to love. On calm blue days when we glide, our wake closing up behind us, it seems that nothing could disturb its sunny serenity. Even the great green scoops of wave created by our passing have their sculptural beauty, and break down from their ridges into a renewed tranquillity. (Strange, that anything so fluid should at the same time contrive to be so marmoreal.) Little rainbows fly from their crests. Happy dolphins, like jokes, cleave the surface. How ingenious of Dionysus, when harassed by pirates, to think of metamorphosising them into dolphins. The whole ocean laughs; I laugh with it.

Then come mysterious currents which rock the ship from below without much visible convulsion. Where do they come from, these secret arteries of the sea, tropical or polar? They are as inexplicable to me as the emotions which rock my own heart. I do not let them appear on the surface but am terribly aware of them beneath. Sometimes, churned by a gale, the waters grow angry and the blue expanse turns black and white, tossing us remorselessly, the waves crashing with a sound as of breaking biscuits, the rain hissing as it obliterates all vision, and again I draw the parallel between the elements and the surprising violence I have discovered in myself.

*   *   *   *

Today, as I write, I am happy. We have been laughing together, comparing remarks overheard amongst our fellow-passengers. I thought I had won the competition with 'I'm awfully afraid, Mr. Carr, that I must confess I do love trippering,' but Laura preferred her contribution of 'I don't care much for Venice, do you, Mrs. Drysdale—so dirty, needs a lick of paint.' We amuse ourselves also with the translations on the menu, this not being an English ship: Dainti Bits, Curried Palmists—what on earth can that be?—Singed sea-wolf, Salmon in Bun, Tre-trunck cak, and Lambkin with Rosemarie, which Laura says sounds very Chaucerian. With such frivolities do we punctuate our days. I suspect that she thinks them salutary for me, who am apt to be too solemn and in need of a play-fellow.

She is a tease, too. She bought me a ridiculous little toy in the shape of a goose that waggles its head with every vibration or draught. 'Set it in front of you on your writing-table,' she said, 'as a reminder of what a goose you are, and of what gooses we all are.'

123

I have obeyed her injunction, as I would always obey her slightest injunction, and as I write these notes the little goose waggles its head at me saying goosey goosey Edmund, what a goose you are.

How dare she tease me thus? No other woman ever dared to make fun of me in this light-hearted way. The other women always attempted to 'understand' me, and I hate being 'understood.' Laura takes a short-cut towards understanding me without saying so.

I much prefer to be given a toy goose with a waggly head than to be asked questions penetrating into what sort of person I really am. But anyhow, how can I know what sort of a person I really am? Who does know? Who ever knows about himself?

Oh Laura, Laura, what a perfect friend and playfellow for me! How happy you make me! How miserable, how desperate! My perfect love, my perfect woman. My missed opportunity. My Laura, my Laura. No, not my Laura. Never to be my Laura. Never, never, never. . . .

*　　*　　*　　*

Yet when we laugh and joke, I can be happy, even exhilarated. I had gone to bed in just such a mood of happy exhilaration, reliant at least on her affection; bitterness had left my soul, as great a relief as the cessation of physical pain. Towards two in the morning I was awakened, not by a sound but by a light, a curious greenish light which filled my cabin and remained constant, as though the beam

124

of a searchlight had been directed against my port-hole. Going to look out, I saw that the whole sky was illuminated; the sea lay glassy calm and lustrous; the dark shape of an island rose in a peak on the horizon. The silence was absolute, except for the faint silky whisper of our own passage through the water. I realised at once that this was an electric storm, and my thoughts flew to Laura: did she sleep with her curtains drawn? Was she missing so rare and weird a spectacle? The confidence of my mood was still upon me, giving me an audacity I should otherwise have lacked.

The corridor was brightly lit, for on a ship the lights are never turned off. Usually there is some figure scurrying down its shiny perspective, but now it was deserted as I made my way along to Laura's cabin. I thought I had never seen her look so lovely as when she opened the door, somewhat startled, a blue silk dressing-gown tightly tied over her pyjamas.

'Oh, it's you,' she said. 'I have been watching the storm. Come out on my balcony.'

'What is so strange about it,' I said after we had leant over the rail for a few moments, 'is the silence. Lightning ought to be accompanied by thunder, however distant. But there is not a sound.'

'It is very beautiful.'

'I was afraid you might not wake, that's why I came.'

'I am glad you came. We shall have seen it together.'

125

I was never nearer to betraying myself. The lightning flickered and then steadied again; it seemed as though the heavens were one vast cavern of light, endless, and the sea endless too, for there was no horizon to divide them. And it seemed to me that love was like that, all radiance and no boundaries. Such, I thought, must be the nature of mystical experience. Time did not exist. Nothing mattered, except that she and I were alone, bathed in this resplendent glory.

'Laura . . .' I said.

'Hush. Don't talk.'

That saved me. I was on the point of betrayal. At the same moment the light began to diminish, symbolically, and she turned away.

'It's over.'

'Yes,' I said, 'it's over.'

*   *   *   *

Nevertheless when I look back in sobriety I find much comfort in that flawless hour. I cling always to the little hints of friendship she gives me, and I had certainly not imagined her saying 'We shall have seen it together.' How was I to interpret that, except as meaning that she was willing, nay, glad to share? And that, in its turn, might mean that she had grown a little fond of me. True, fondness was not all that I could have asked of her, but a beggar cannot afford to despise a farthing. If I could believe that I had found the slightest favour in her eyes!

126

Do I deceive myself into thinking that her manner has imperceptibly changed? Wishes are great persuaders. All my old doubts return to torment me. Supposing I had not found her alone? (But you did, you fool, you did.) Supposing she had looked embarrassed, and, thanking me for my trouble, had shut a half-opened door upon me? (She did not, you fool; she let you in.) And again I say to myself, two o'clock is deep into the night, a lover might well have come and gone by then, and I none the wiser. This way madness lies. Let me rather think of her as good and kind, sweetness itself, gay and serious by turns, brave—I am sure she is brave—generous in her giving. Ah, if she loved, how good she would be, in sickness or distress.

*   *   *   *

Whatever happens, she must never guess. The Egyptian answered wisely, when asked what he had hidden under his cloak, 'It is hidden under my cloak, that thou mayest not know what it is.'

*   *   *   *

> Alas, my heart! what passions do thee rend!
> Thus was I not, but thus am I become
> And thus I fear persist until my end
> And persecute my dearest closest friend
> With cries unworthy of the love I bear.
>
> Thus did the Moor of Venice madly tear
> More than his heart, his very soul apart,
> In black suspicion of white innocence . . .

127

Oh no, it's no good. Why do I attempt to write love poems for Laura? I can't even find the necessary rhymes, I can't even parody an Elizabethan sonnet. It's no good; I'm no good; I'm finished, done for.

*   *   *   *

At least he does not call her by her Christian name; they are formally Mrs. Drysdale and Colonel Dalrymple. Perhaps this is only camouflage for public consumption; ship-board acquaintances of our generation do not readily drop into Christian names, whatever the lax young may do. I observe them carefully, to see if their eyes ever meet in the complicity of a private joke, but so far have not caught them out. Perhaps she has cautioned him. She may have said, 'Be careful in front of Edmund Carr, he is shrewd, and might guess.' I cannot forget or forgive myself that sneer I let fall when I met them coming out of her cabin, and was afraid that I had given myself away. I feel sure she picked it up; she misses very little.

*   *   *   *

The end cannot be very far off now; the doctor gave me two to four months at the outside, and we have been away for nearly three. Besides, I have felt for the first time some twinges of pain, which he told me to expect as a warning. I forced him to tell me the whole truth, in detail. He assured me that these twinges would neither incapacitate me nor cause me more than a momentary wince, but they would indicate that the disease was reaching some vital part and I must be prepared for the worst. I cannot regard it as the worst; the worst was when I realised that I could never, however wildly, however hopelessly, aspire to Laura. That, and not the loss of life, was the supreme renunciation. I daresay that in the goodness of her heart she might have yielded to me out of pity; it was not upon those terms that I wanted her. And now, when she seems to soften towards me, the prohibition is even harder to bear.

What was it she said? That if she found herself stricken—and I think she meant under sentence of death—she would try to accept the verdict without rebellion. And so, at times, I do.

It is not for nothing that the Samurai have chosen for their truest symbol the fragile cherry blossom. Like a petal dropping in the morning sunlight and floating serenely to earth, so must the fearless detach himself from life, silent and inwardly unafraid.

$$* \qquad * \qquad * \qquad *$$

I have just had a most puzzling conversation with Laura and do not know what to make of it. If she were another woman, I should think that she was trying to lead me on, but with her such an idea is untenable. What contributes to my mystification is my inability to isolate any phrase, any question, which could not have occurred in our talk in the past; it is something subtle, not concrete, that I am trying to pin down. Perhaps I can best express it by saying that sometimes she appears to be on the

129

brink of going further, and then draws back, irresolute. Yet I must not attach too much importance to her indecision, for I have long been provokingly acquainted with her reluctance to advance deeper into intimacy, whether in self-defence or out of respect for another's privacy I have never been able to determine. Probably both. Nevertheless I remain faintly (not strongly) under the impression that there is something she wishes to learn from me, or possibly something of which she wishes to apprise me. Does it mean that I might be of help to her in any way? How gladly would I give her my service. But she must hasten. I have not much time left.

I cannot compare her to the wild bird one seeks to tame, for the simile would be inappropriate: it is not I who essay to entice her, but rather she who with no inducement walks round me in alternately narrowing and widening circles. Yet the image is recurrent in my mind.

> Like as a dove the proffered corn refuseth,
> Yet ever nearer to the hand approacheth,
> So doth my love . . .

I cannot remember how it goes on, and alas I have no corn to proffer.

*   *   *   *

She opened the conversation by asking if I realised that we were more than half-way through our journey.

'I do indeed, Laura; I no longer know which is East and which is West.'

130

'You have enjoyed it?'

I think of the miserable hours spent going round and round in the intricacies of jealousy, and reply truthfully,

'There have been times which I have enjoyed very much indeed.'

'What do you look back on with the greatest pleasure?'

I countered.

'What do you?'

Her reply was unexpected, for it was the one I should have given myself.

'The evening we spent in that little house on the Spanish island.'

I suppose I stared at her in astonishment, for she went on,

'It was so peaceful, Edmund; so altogether satisfying. I scarcely knew where I had got to; I only had a curious feeling of having come home.'

Then, as though she had said too much, she added, 'And then there was the night of the electric storm, when we watched it from my balcony, only that was different: more exciting and somehow more dangerous. Of course I knew it wasn't really dangerous at all.'

Oh Laura! didn't you?

'I feel flattered,' I said as lightly as I could, 'that two of the peaks of your enjoyment should have been moments you shared with me.'

'And now we shall go back,' she said, 'and pick up our lives where we dropped them. You will be

131

at the heart of things again, important things, and I shall let myself into my flat and find that it has been spring-cleaned and all my books put back in the wrong places or upside down. We shall meet from time to time at the houses of our friends, and perhaps sometimes when you have an hour to spare you will come and call on me. You haven't often done so in the past, but then we hadn't had this journey together. Do you remember, once, not long before we sailed, you rang me up to ask if you might come round?'

I did remember; it was the evening of the day I had had that interview with my doctor.

'Were you surprised?' I asked.

'Well, you had never been to my flat before, of your own accord. Only by invitation.'

'And that not very often, and always with other people there. I had a sudden idea that I should like to see you alone.'

She looked at me gravely, but did not ask why.

'I hope you will sometimes have the same idea again. But I know how busy you are, and shan't expect it.'

'And I know how much in request you are—so many friends—a lady of fashion.'

'Edmund, that's unkind. I believe you could say very unkind things, if you were so minded. Just because you have met me in a social way you imagine that my life is one long train of frivolity. You would be surprised if you knew how much time I spend by myself.'

'I suspect also that you have many charitable occupations of which I know nothing.'

'Oh, I sit on a few committees.' I could see that she did not intend to enlarge upon that. Juvenile delinquents? prisoners? refugees? I wondered what. 'I like being by myself,' she continued. 'Don't you find that people take so much out of one, that one has a need to replenish? We might occasionally go to a concert,' she added inconsequently.

'Or spend a day in the country,' I said, cold at the heart before this unrealisable project.

'I should love that above all things. It will be spring when we get home. We could motor down into Kent or Sussex, walk over the Downs, have our supper at some inn, and drive back late to London. But again, could you ever spare the time?'

'Nothing but death itself could prevent me from accepting such an invitation.'

She laughed.

'I didn't expect such gallantry. Very well: I shall hold you to it. It would be a pity, don't you agree, if we were to allow our friendship to lapse back into mere acquaintance? One hasn't so many friends in this world.'

'I always imagined that yours were legion.'

'Very superficially. I had one close friend in my life once, a woman, but she died some years ago and since then I have never cared to make another.'

I said nothing, feeling that any expression of sympathy would be out of place.

'What I like about you, Edmund,' she said, as

133

though answering my unspoken thought, 'is your reticence. You never blunder. I sometimes think I could talk to you as I would to another woman. I didn't tell you the whole truth just now,' she added. 'I said my friend died. She was, in fact, done to death in France by the Milice.'

'Laura!'

'Yes, by her own countrymen. They had a reluctance to shooting women outright, but they didn't mind torturing them. She, my friend, wasn't strong, and she died as a result. I managed to escape myself. I wish now that I hadn't. I can't help feeling that I betrayed her—and the others—though of course I know that it wouldn't really have made any difference.'

I ventured to ask,

'You were working for the Resistance?'

'Yes. My friend was French, she had an estate in the Corrèze, we were able to shelter quite a number of escaping Englishmen, airmen mostly, who had been shot down or baled out. We got them away eventually over the Pyrenees. But in the end we were caught.'

'And you?'

'Some peasants hid me in the maquis.'

She did not seem disposed to say any more, leaving me to fill in the details for myself, but I remained with the impression that she had deliberately forced herself to this scanty revelation. Was it because she wished to draw closer to me? I hoped that I might believe so.

134

Today she reverted to the subject of loneliness.

'When I lived with Tommy,' she said, 'I was often lonely though seldom alone. We led what most people would consider a gay, full life; to me it seemed empty. I told you, didn't I, that I liked being alone? Almost a physical necessity. But there is a great difference between solitude and loneliness. One is weak, Edmund. I have come to believe that even the strongest, the most self-sufficient, need one other person in their lives from whom nothing is concealed, neither the most important things nor the most trivial. Someone with whom at the end of the day one can sit over the fire and talk or be silent as the fancy moves one.'

'Supposing one lost that person?'

'Hostages to Fortune? Well, I've been through it, so I know. I had that kind of relationship with the friend I was telling you about. And yet I don't know. Perhaps a relationship between two women must always be incomplete—unless, I suppose, they have Lesbian inclinations which I don't happen to share. Then, or so I have been given to understand, the concord may approach perfection. You see, there is a kind of free-masonry between women— and no doubt between men also—which makes up for the more elemental excitement of the sex-war. Also, women have many petty interests in common, which would bore a man. Clothes, shops!' she said with a smile.

I love her when she suddenly smiles, serious one moment and amused the next.

135

'There must always be a snag, though,' she went on. 'I knew two women, Lesbians, who lived for years together in a harmony more idyllic than the majority of marriages. One of them used to confide in me, I can't think why, except that she saw I was interested. And I *was* interested; it was an aspect of love I had never come across. You look sceptical, but I assure you that it was love, deep, sincere, and in its way beautiful.'

'What was the snag, then?'

'Jealousy. You say you don't know the meaning of the word. These two knew it, in all its cruellest refinements, especially the one who made a confidante of me; she was the more masculine of the two. You see, if a man is jealous of a woman, he at least meets his rival on level ground, man to man; but if a woman is jealous of a woman, she enters into an unfair competition with the other sex; she is always afraid that the natural thing will conquer in the end. In this case the other woman, Lucy, the feminine one, was highly attractive to men, and although I don't believe she ever responded there was always the danger that she might some day do so. I can't tell you what torments my poor friend went through. She would seize upon every tiny circumstance and construe it according to her suspicions. She hated herself for it, for at heart she was really rather a noble creature, but that's the devil of jealousy: it transforms people. Tommy was jealous of me—possessive—but that was simple and straightforward and never worried me; it hadn't

136

got this cruel twist in it. I used to try and reassure that wretched woman, who was going just the right way to ruin their two lives, but although she would wring her hands and cry, "I know! I know all that," I could no more convince her than I could argue that iron stanchion into walking about. The worst of it was that people fed her mistrust, whether out of malice or sheer unawareness I never could make out. They would say that this man or that appeared to have taken a great fancy to Lucy: did she think there was anything in it? Then there would be another terrible scene. I really thought that she would end by wearing Lucy down and driving her into marriage with some quiet kind man in self-defence, and possibly a suicide thrown in, but the rest of the story is quite tame, and so far as I know they are peacefully ageing together and floating into calm waters.'

'A cautionary tale. What an expenditure of energy, and all for nothing.'

'If I loved,' said Laura, looking at me with a severity that was almost a challenge, 'I should be utterly faithful, and I should presume the same fidelity in the other person. In small things as well as great, unquestioning.'

'And if you found out . . . anything you resented?'

'I should pack up and go.'

*   *   *   *

Now I ask myself why in Heaven's name she should have taken to talking to me like this. I check off the points: the continuance of our own friendship, some recollections of her past, loneliness, jealousy including that red herring of a story about the two women, and her own view of fidelity and love. How can I make a synthesis of all these elements? There is only one conclusion that I can come to.

She values our friendship; so far, so good. She wishes to pursue it when we get home and makes little plans for a day in the country, when we shall motor back to London after supper. Very innocent. So far, so good, again. She contrasts solitude with loneliness, and indicates that we all stand in need of one complete relationship in our life, implying thereby that she feels the lack of it in hers. Then she goes on to caution me against the destructive power of jealousy—and this is where I come to the first hurdle. I once informed her, truthfully at the time, that I did not know the meaning of the word, a remark she has not forgotten. But, since she forgets nothing, she must also remember the snarl I let out when I met Dalrymple emerging from her cabin and which I could see she had correctly interpreted. From here on, taking the hurdle, logic leads me straight down the course. She is trying to tell me that she intends to import Dalrymple into her life, maybe as a husband, maybe as a lover; it comes to the same; she does not want to lose sight of me altogether, yet is honest enough to warn me that neither will she tolerate jealous spite nor permit me any licence beyond the limits of normal friendship. It seems to me that these deductions are inescapable.

Of course it may not be Dalrymple at all, but some man unknown with whom she has an understanding in England. It would be characteristic of her uprightness to clarify the situation in advance, taking it in good time now that we are homeward bound. What does it matter to me, Dalrymple or another? I cannot believe that with that ingenuous Colonel she would find the companionship she desires. Laura who is so clear-sighted must surely see that? Or is love sufficiently unaccountable for her to delude herself? Could anything but love, or at any rate a strong attraction, induce her to spend so many hours in his uninspiring company? No, it must be love, it must be Dalrymple; he is always at her side, and if he finds me there before him he turns away with a scowl. I have seen it. No doubt she makes up for his disappointment afterwards; I shall not waste my pity upon him by thinking that perhaps the poor devil goes through the same torment as I.

She never mentions him to me, a fact which I regard as most suggestive. But then what do I not regard as suggestive in my present diseased state of mind?

Why do I not question her outright? Because I dread the answer.

*   *   *   *

A dire thought strikes me: supposing she wants

to ask my advice? Not that I imagine she is in the habit of consulting anybody—she is far too self-reliant—but she is quite alone and I cannot help knowing that she values my opinion. I think also, humbly, that she has developed a certain fondness for me, as for a faithful dog. She may also reflect that a man is better equipped to form a judgement on another man; no, not better perhaps, I used the wrong word, but from a different angle. Although she knows that I now have my reasons for resentment against the Colonel, she may pay me the compliment of believing me capable of objectivity. Hence all this preparation about jealousy and so forth. What should I do if she spoke? Could I bring myself to answer calmly and in her best interests? Could I say 'He is a good fellow, trustworthy, and so long as you realise his limitations you might do worse?' Or would all my resolution break down in a storm of rage? Would all my own desperate hopeless love come pouring out?

No! no! no! the thing is unthinkable. It only shows what a plight I have come to that I should have entertained the idea for a moment.

*　　　*　　　*　　　*

I have not been feeling well today; those little naggings of pain were fairly frequent, though in themselves inconsiderable. I kept to my cabin, afraid of betraying myself by a sudden flinch, and also—shall I confess it?—prompted further by a faint hope that Laura might notice my absence and

140

take steps to enquire. Thus do I crave for any little sign of affection she may show me.

A knock on my door.

'What's the matter, Edmund? You never appeared all morning, and you weren't at luncheon. Oh, so you're not ill,' she said, seeing that I was up and fully dressed.

'I had a bad headache, a touch of the sun I expect. Better now. How good of you to bother.' Just because I had been feeling ill, and was a little frightened, some foolish impulse made me add, 'You might have sent the Colonel to find out.'

'Edmund, you are silly about the Colonel, always having digs at that poor man. You used to like him; you told me so yourself. I should never have believed you were so vindictive. It all dates from the day he scolded you for letting me go into that market; you've never forgiven him. And he did apologise.'

So she does not suspect me of jealousy after all, in spite of the incident at her cabin door. Or is she so clever a woman as to want to spare my pride? If so, I can double-cross her ingenuity. Men, though women do not believe it, can see through women sometimes.

She looked round my cabin, so bare in comparison with hers, and caught sight of my dressing-gown swinging from a hook.

'Your dressing-gown is torn; give it to me, I'll take it away and mend it for you.'

'No!' I could not bear to let her go so soon. 'You

can't be seen walking down the passage with my old Paisley over your arm. If you insist on mending it at all, do it in here.'

In a moment she was back with a little box full of cottons and things; sat on the edge of my bed, and began to sew. I watched her threading her needle, snipping the thread with a minute pair of scissors, examining the triangular rent to see how she could best set about it. Her delicate fingers flicked the needle in and out. I remembered how other women had irritatingly tried to interfere with my belongings, and how surly a reception they had got.

It was very peaceful; I felt better; pain seemed remote.

'What a charmingly domestic scene,' I said. 'But you haven't got an egg.'

'An egg?'

'My mother had a wooden egg that she used for darning socks.' I could almost hear the lid of the saucepan rattling in my mother's kitchen . . .

'Of course! My Nannie had one too. Are you sure I am not disturbing you?'

'You do me all the good in the world by being here.'

'You are telling me the truth, Edmund, aren't you? It was nothing worse than a headache, a touch of the sun?'

I thought she scrutinised me rather sharply.

'What else should it be? A mere nothing. I have quite recovered.'

142

'You wouldn't tell me a lie?'

Oh Laura, if only you knew how many lies I have told you.

'I should hate to have to tell you a lie.' That, at any rate, is true.

'And you would like to please me?'

'I would do anything to please you.'

'Then will you lie down and sleep it off for the rest of the afternoon? You don't look well, you know. Listen to my professional advice; I told you I was a nurse once.'

'Sister Laura?'

'You can call me Sister if you like, so long as you do what I say. Lie down on your bed and let me cover you over. I have mended your dressing-gown —a labour of love if not of skill. Have you any aspirin?'

'Somewhere . . . I'll look for it . . .' but she was into my washing-place and returned with two tablets and a glass of water.

'Drink this. Crunch the tablets up, they'll work quicker. You haven't taken any already, by the way? Never thought of it! Well, take these and then go to sleep.'

'Laura, I suppose you realise I would have murdered any other woman for less than this?'

She laid my dressing-gown over me, and then to my intense astonishment bent down and kissed me very lightly on the forehead.

'Go to sleep.'

*   *   *   *

143

How willingly would I go to sleep for ever if I could have her at my side. Even as it is, her scent pervades my cabin and deceives me into imagining her physical presence; I shut my eyes, the better to fancy that she was still there, but the aspirin beyond whose reach I so far am did its work and I slept, slept to dream that she loved me, the nearest that I shall ever come to the unrealisable. I know now that the end must be very near; all the little symptoms I was told to look out for are becoming recurrent. Before long I must throw this diary, Laura's gift, into the sea.

*   *   *   *

'Tell me, Edmund, what made you embark on this journey? You said once that you had never travelled before.'

I could not reply that it was in order to spend my last weeks near her.

'I thought I deserved a holiday.'

She persisted.

'That day you rang up and asked to come and see me, a very short time before we started, you said nothing about it. Yet I think I remember telling you then that I was about to set off.'

I writhed under this dangerous cross-examination.

'I don't remember—it must have been a coincidence—I probably had not made up my mind. Yes, that's right: it was a sudden decision. I felt tired, stale. I wanted to get away.'

144

'You were lucky to get a passage at such short notice.'

'Very lucky. There was a cancellation.' This was partially true, but knowing that some berths were always held in reserve, I had also used the influence of my paper to pull strings. 'Our Special Correspondent writes . . .' That sort of bribe.

'I think, though, that I had told you the name of my ship?'

'I must have forgotten. Now if I were really as gallant as you have sometimes twitted me with being, I should pretend that I had done it on purpose.'

'To give me a surprise? You certainly did. I couldn't believe my eyes when I saw you come on board at Genoa. I thought it must be your double.'

'Talking of doubles,' I said, for I was anxious to get her off the subject, 'did you know that there was only one place in the world where coconuts grow double? Like Siamese twins. It is in a valley in one of the Seychelles, which General Gordon firmly believed to be the original Garden of Eden.'

'I thought the Garden of Eden was supposed to be somewhere in Mesopotamia.'

'Yes, but there is also a theory that, owing to a continental drift, part of Asia broke away and floated over towards the coast of Africa. Isn't it a fact that certain Asiatic flora are found and will flourish nowhere but in India and Madagascar? Thousands of miles apart. This curious occurrence cannot otherwise be explained.'

Laura surprises me sometimes; she said, 'There is

145

also a little primula which grows only on one of the Aleutian islands.'

'How do you know that?'

'Colonel Dalrymple told me.'

*   *   *   *

It is true that he has a way of coming out with odd little bits of information. I suppose that that is partly what renders him attractive in Laura's eyes. For the hundredth time I wish that I could dislike the man I hate.

*   *   *   *

It is not only jealousy that makes me hate him, but the despicable actions into which it drives me. Most unjustly, I blame them upon him. That I, of all men, should turn spy! Lying awake, I listen for sounds in the night, and have opened my door half expecting to see a figure retreating down the corridor. I never have, but then I return to my bed cursing the rubber-soled, rope-soled noiseless shoes one wears on a ship, which would enable him to pass my door a hundred times unheard. I hate him for the sheer vulgarity of my suspicions, quite as much as I hate myself.

I look back over every circumstance and interpret it according to my altered disposition. I thought him sympathetic, did I, when he shared my anxiety over Laura's illness? Fool that I was! his solicitude was not as disinterested as I thought. It was kind of him, was it, to suggest that I should write her a note

146

of enquiry? I see now that he was using me as a go-between. He wanted to know, and it was an easy way of discreetly finding out. Why, though, did he not write himself? Clearly because they had not yet arrived at their understanding, whereas I was the safe old friend, a dog that Laura was pleased to pat. And so I go round and round.

*   *   *   *

Laura continues to persecute me, now when I feel too uneasy to stand up to much persecution or to meet it with the evasive banter I usually attempt. She seems determined to find out more about me, which is so unlike her usual practice that I find myself constantly looking round for her motive. There is something at the back of her mind that I cannot fathom. Sometimes I think that it is a kindly anxiety about my health, for she shakes her head at me and says I do not look well; sometimes I think it is merely a feminine desire to run my life for me, the last infirmity I should ever have suspected of her.

I am at sea in more ways than one.

She asks me about my childhood, and in a sense I find it rather soothing to talk about the past when one has so little future. Thus in extreme old age do people revert to forgotten scenes with a vividness of memory that has no counterpart in their present. What does it matter if today is Wednesday or Thursday, when one can recall the glow of building a snow-man and sticking a pipe into his mouth? Our cottage door had a latch you lifted by pulling a shoe-string; to this day I can hear the familiar click.

'But why do you want to know, Laura?'

'I like making a picture of your background. When we first met in London you floated in a void; I knew none of the steps by which you had arrived where you were. Edmund Carr, brilliant and successful and sought after; an agreeable man to meet socially. Try to see yourself from the outside, as I saw you.'

'And how do you suppose I saw you?'

'Oh, just as one of those women to whom you had to make polite conversation.'

Does she wish me to pay her conventional compliments?

'If you remember,' I said, 'I once invited you to come to Kew with me. Had you but known it, that was a very unusual thing for me to do.'

'Had you no women friends, then? Real friends, I mean.'

'Not real enough for me to want to spend the afternoon with them.'

'I feel very much flattered, Edmund, and I really mean that. May I ask you an indiscreet question? You never married?'

'Goodness no, Laura; did you imagine I was a widower, or divorced?'

'I just wondered. I won't ask you why.'

'Probably because I never met anybody for whom I should have been willing to sacrifice my independence.'

'We hold the same views on a good many subjects

I think: I have told you my own rather unorthodox ideas on marriage. But as one grows older one has to modify one's theories. What about old age? Have you ever seriously contemplated the . . . the desolation of finding oneself quite alone in the world? No one to care for? No one to care for you?'

'It seems to weigh on your mind. Surely you are too young to begin anticipating such a situation?'

'If one waited too long,' she said slowly, 'one might have missed the opportunity.'

*   *   *   *

So now I know. All my apprehensions have resolved themselves into one cold certainty. There was a purpose behind everything she said, only she broke off short before coming to the conclusion. She wants to confide in me, but cannot quite bring herself to the point, her natural reticence still stronger than her desire to impart her fermenting secret.

I ought to help her; I *will* help her; it will be the last sacrifice I can lay at her feet. I am determined not to break down now that I have stood out so long.

> Forget not yet the tried intent
> Of such a truth as I have meant,
> My great travail so gladly spent,
>   Forget not yet.
>
> Forget not yet the great assays,
> The cruel wrong, the scornful ways,
> The painful patience in denays,
>   Forget not yet.

Forget not yet, forget not this,
How long ago hath been and is
The mind that never meant amiss,
    Forget not yet.

Forget not then thine own approved
The which so long hath thee so loved,
Whose steadfast faith yet never moved,
    Forget not this.

*   *   *   *

We were sitting alone on the upper deck after
dinner; the Colonel for once was playing Bridge
with some other people. The place and the hour
could not have been more propitious.

My opening was crude.

'Laura,' I said, 'we have talked much, one way
and another, but there is one subject we have
seldom touched on, except obliquely: love.'

She looked startled, as well she might.

'I told you once what I thought of it and its rare,
possible perfection,' she said. 'I didn't think you
attributed great importance to love as a factor in life.
Men don't usually dwell on it much, do they, unless
they happen to be in love themselves at the
moment?'

'Which you assumed I wasn't, and never had been?'

'Well, I wasn't so naïve as not to suppose you had
had your passing fancies.'

'How right you were. Passing is what we journal-
ists call the operative word.'

'You also told me you had never met anyone to
whom you were prepared to sacrifice your inde-

pendence, so what other conclusion could I come to? Your independence may have been precious, but when one is in love one does not calculate.'

'Non-calculation sometimes leads to lethal mistakes.'

'If you mean that I should never have married Tommy . . .'

'I take it that one does not commit the same mistake twice, not unless one is a film-star with a positive passion for divorce. No. But one would not commit it unless one was very sure that it wasn't one—and when one is in love one isn't always able to judge.'

'If one had thought very long and seriously . . .'

'Very long—how long?'

'Oh, say two months. Beginning with a great liking, that deepened day by day, but remained placid and platonic, until . . .'

'Yes? Until?'

'Until one realised that one began to look round for the . . . the person when he wasn't there; felt incomplete in his absence; expanded when he came; looked for little signs of his sympathy; was easily happy, and as easily cast down and tremulous; lived in bewilderment; did not put two and two together, until one suddenly said to oneself, "What is this? What does it mean?" '

'And then?'

'Then one knows—blindingly. It takes some courage to face; one's submission is so appalling, so improbable. One had thought oneself so safe, and

151

there one is, lying on the ground with a lion standing over one. And then everything becomes invested
with an immense significance—what is that drug
that heightens every sense?'

'Mescalin.'

'With one part of oneself one knows that it doesn't
make sense—why should one single out one person
rather than another? Reasonably one knows that he
is neither the handsomest nor the cleverest nor the
most faultless in the world, but reason has become
a foreign language one does not understand. All
the novelists that ever wrote have failed to explain
what brings about this strange . . . electricity that
sparks; what sets it off in the first instance; they
describe the effects but not the cause. Love, fondness,
devotion, one can comprehend; but not this extraordinary nature of *in love-ness*; you see that I separate
them, though the one may contain the other, and
love may outlast *in* love. One hopes it will; sometimes one knows it will. But there's plenty of time
to think about that later; it seems very homespun
compared with the incandescent flame. For the time
being nothing matters but the one thing. *Parceque
c'était lui ; parceque c'était moi.'*

She was flushed; her eloquence seemed to be
dictated by something outside herself.

'One's life becomes like this ship, all lit up in the
midst of the darkness. Think how beautiful she
must look, to watchers on the shore—the rows of
lights, the great arclights illuminating her white
sides. No, that is too abstract, for love is compounded

of many elements; there is the blaze of light, but there is also the detail, the infinite tenderness of discovery. A tone of the voice, a turn of the head, a gesture of the hand, all hitherto unremarked but now how revealing! And to observe from afar, unseen oneself, and to say in one's heart, "I love you, darling!" '

'Are you quite sure,' I said as gently as I could, 'that you are not confusing love with physical attraction? It can be very misleading, you know—a sort of masquerading proxy, a Doppel-gänger.'

'Do you not think that by a certain age and with a certain amount of experience one may become capable of distinguishing? I have not been speaking of calf-love. I have been speaking of an astonishing thing which comes upon one in later life, when all such thoughts had been put away as an impossibility, and one believed rather sadly that fulfilment was nowhere to be found in this world. One is well aware of all the flickering deceptions—after all, one is made of flesh and blood, and there will have been incidents over the years, like your passing fancies—oh yes, the flesh can be a very convincing cheat. I know that. One has even known a tremor of it, ridiculously, meeting the eyes of a stranger across a restaurant. But when one has had time for reflection, and even in one's intervals of sanity time enough for a close examination—a study of the person, I mean, his nature, character, climate of mind and so on—when you have discovered him to be sensitive and delicate of spirit, strong of mind but fastidious and imaginative, a sort of *poète manqué*—don't you agree that one can be sure, sure, sure?'

Poor darling, she must be besotted indeed if she can think of the Colonel in those terms.

'Laura,' I said, 'forgive me if I seem impertinent; you need not answer if you don't want to; but are you speaking personally or theoretically?'

There was a long pause. Her face was almost hidden from me in the shadows. She bent down to do something to her shoe.

'Personally,' she said then. 'I have been wanting to tell you this for some time, but although I tried you gave me no encouragement.'

'And now what do you want me to give you? My advice?'

She turned to me, and I saw that her eyes were lit with all the radiance of love. And not her eyes only; her whole being dissolved into a softness, a readiness, a loveliness of assent.

'Your advice?' she said. 'Well, I suppose you are my best friend. What is your advice?'

At all costs I must save her from falling into irretrievable error.

'You are not a conventional woman,' I said; 'your appearance belies you. You have told me your views on marriage, your insistence on individual liberty. To achieve that, you must have the agreement of the other person. I cannot believe that you would get it, or at least you might obtain all kinds of promises, given in the blindness of the moment—a man in love will say anything he is asked—but

154

they would very soon be broken. Try it out first, Laura, before you find yourself committed for good.'

'You mean, take him as my lover?'

'If you must. Assuage your passion,' I said savagely, 'and then see what's left behind.'

'But I told you I was so sure,' she said, a pitiable note coming into her voice. I hated to be responsible for her elation fading.

'How can one be sure, when one is besotted? Your conception of marriage—I say *marriage*, not the lover-relationship—includes companionship and an affinity of outlook. Something durable. Would you find that, I ask you, with Dalrymple?'

'*Dalrymple?*' she said. 'The Colonel? Oh, you fool, Edmund,' she said. 'You blind fool!'

*　　　*　　　*　　　*

I cannot think, I dare not think. . . . Folly, folly, folly!

She got up and went, leaving me alone with the lighted ship in the night.

How shall I meet her tomorrow?

Shall I

*　　　*　　　*　　　*

Edmund Carr was found dead in his cabin the morning after this conversation had taken place. He had fallen forward on to his table, his diary open at the page where he had recorded these last broken-off words. The ship's doctor, on the strength of the medical report found in Carr's wallet, had no

155

hesitation in signing a certificate of death from natural causes.

Carr had also included a note to the effect that he wished to be buried at sea. These instructions were duly carried out in the Pacific Ocean, latitude 25° south, longitude 175° west. A canister of lighted petrol was thrown in after him, briefly to mark the spot, and those on board watched it burning as the ship proceeded on her way, until the flame died down and nothing more was seen.